Once in the Saddle

Center Point
Large Print

Also by L.P. Holmes and available from
Center Point Large Print:

The Crimson Hills
Free Winds Blow West
Orphans of Gunswift Graze
The Sunset Trail

**This Large Print Book carries the
Seal of Approval of N.A.V.H.**

ONCE
in the
SADDLE

A Western Story

L. P. HOLMES

CENTER POINT LARGE PRINT
THORNDIKE, MAINE

This Center Point Large Print edition
is published in the year 2017 by arrangement with
Golden West Literary Agency.

Once in the Saddle, the author's title for this story, first
appeared under the title "Redwood Country" as a four-
part serial in *Ranch Romances* (2nd November Number:
1/23/51–1st January Number: 1/4/52). Copyright © 1951
by Best Books, Inc. Copyright © renewed 1979 by
L. P. Holmes. Copyright © 2013 by Golden West
Literary Agency for restored material.

The text of this Large Print edition is unabridged.
In other aspects, this book may vary
from the original edition.
Printed in the United States of America
on permanent paper.
Set in 16-point Times New Roman type.

ISBN: 978-1-68324-626-8 (hardcover)
ISBN: 978-1-68324-630-5 (paperback)

Library of Congress Cataloging-in-Publication Data

Names: Holmes, L. P. (Llewellyn Perry), 1895-1988. author.
Title: Once in the saddle : a western story / L.P. Holmes.
Description: Center Point Large Print edition. | Thorndike, Maine :
    Center Point Large Print, 2017.
Identifiers: LCCN 2017041671| ISBN 9781683246268
    (hardcover : alk. paper) | ISBN 9781683246305 (pbk. : alk. paper)
Subjects: LCSH: Ranchers—Fiction. | Rangelands—West (U.S.)—
    Fiction. | Forests and forestry—Fiction. | Coast redwood—Fiction. |
    Cattle Stealing—Fiction. | Large type books. | GSAFD: Western stories.
Classification: LCC PS3515.O4448 O53 2017 | DDC 813/.54—dc23
LC record available at https://lccn.loc.gov/2017041671

Once in the Saddle

Chapter One

It was an eerie, almost frightening thing to watch the great redwood tree die. This, thought Wade Stagmire, was truly a giant in a land of giants. It stood well along toward the far end of the ragged slash area that spread its ugly scar across the northern flank of this ridge. Many other trees had already been logged from the area; their stumps stood everywhere. Now the big fellow of the grove was being prepared for death.

The comparative open of the slash had burst upon Stagmire abruptly. For the better part of two days he'd been riding through the dim and spectral aisles of a brooding forest that had seemed endless. He had searched for definite trails where there had been none. He had climbed ridges and crossed them and dropped down into cañons beyond. He had followed winding, narrow flats along the banks of cold and hurrying streams and pushed through great patches of giant ferns growing head high to a tall man. Always he'd tried to work west, steadily west.

Last night, supperless, he'd slept at the base of what he thought must surely be the biggest tree in the world. Then, in the chill, filtering dawn of this day, he'd climbed still another ridge, to follow along it until suddenly the interminable forest gave way before him and he was in this slash where morning's sunlight lay clear and golden and where lifted the sounds of men at work.

From the vantage point of his saddle, Stagmire, a tall man in his own right, could look clearly across the litter of the slash to the base of the towering redwood tree. By comparison, the little group of loggers working about the base of the tree were Lilliputian figures, mere human insects, intent upon this giant's destruction. The measured whine of the falling saw seemed to hold a hungry snarl.

The fall, Stagmire saw, would be upslope, for he could mark the rough bed that had been cleared to receive the tree. Now, though plain animal hunger was a gnawing ache within him, he was prepared to watch the finish of this thing. He thumbed a limp tobacco sack from the pocket of his faded, ragged shirt, sifted a last pinch of crumbling grains from it into a brown paper, tossed the sack away, and thought cynically that when a man was down to his last cigarette, a thin one at that, then indeed was the condition of his affairs really desperate. He scratched a match, held it briefly to the tip of the cigarette, and drew the tangy smoke deeply into his lungs. It brought some comfort, but was no substitute for the real food he craved.

A few yards ahead of Stagmire was a piled-up tangle of brush and limbs, the trimmings from another tree that had been felled at some time past. Now, from just beyond the tangle, a man's voice lifted in a shout.

"How much longer, Farwell?"

One of the group at the base of the tree turned and gave deep-voiced answer.

"Any time now, Mister Tedrow. It's beginning to talk!"

Wade Stagmire stirred his ribby mount to movement and rode around the end of the pile of trimmings. He reined up with a small start of surprise, touching the brim of his battered old Stetson. Here were two people, sitting on a stump, and one of them was a girl.

"Sorry," said Stagmire briefly. "Didn't mean to bother. But I'm a stranger in a strange land and could use a few directions."

They looked him over for a moment in silence, seeing a long-limbed man in worn, ragged clothes, a man leaned down to gauntness from far travel and too many missed meals. His jaw was sharply angled and solid, smudged now with a bristle of whiskers, and his eyes were deep-set beneath slightly frowning brows. Cool blue the eyes were, and direct as he spoke.

The man on the stump finally asked: "Directions to where?"

Stagmire shrugged. "Anywhere there is food.

9

A cattle ranch would suit best, if there is such in this country?"

"Grubliner, eh?"

A glint showed briefly in Stagmire's eyes and a faint flush touched his face. "Could be. But not from choice."

There had been a sting, a thread of contempt, in the way the man on the stump had spoken. He was a big man, and under the red-and-black checked Mackinaw he wore, his shoulders bulked heavily. His face was clean-shaven, florid, and his eyes were on the pale side. He was bare-headed, with a big shock of tawny hair. A handsome man, in a virile, physical sort of way. But his lips held the faint curl of arrogance that absolute authority gives to some men.

The girl stirred, threw a glance that held some censure at the man beside her, then looked at Stagmire. "There is the beginning of a little valley down there to the north," she said, pointing. "Follow it and you'll come to old Gib Dawson's Anchor Ranch."

Her voice was low and cool and clear and fitted her perfectly, Stagmire thought. He thought also that here was as pretty a girl as he'd ever seen. Her hair was raven black, her eyebrows the same. But her eyes were gray, a warm and shining gray, and natural color bloomed in her cheeks. Her mouth was generous, sweetly curved, and softly red. She had on a plaid wool skirt, trim laced boots, and a scarlet Mackinaw, the upturned collar of which framed the tapered perfection of her face.

Stagmire couldn't keep his admiration from his eyes, and the girl, seeing it, showed deepening color. Stagmire touched his hat again.

"Ma'am, I'm obliged."

The tawny-haired man had not missed the appreciation of the girl's beauty in Stagmire's glance, so now he spoke roughly.

"You got the directions you wanted, so there's nothing to keep you here. You're on privately owned property, anyhow."

Stagmire looked the fellow up and down, a thread of sharp anger beginning to work in him. But before he could speak again, a shouted word echoed across the slash, stirring in its implication.

"Timber-r-r!"

The girl jumped down from the stump, stood staring wide-eyed at the towering redwood tree. "It's going, Ruel!" she cried. "It's going! And I feel that this is a wicked thing. . . ."

Stagmire's glance followed that of the girl's. The great tree still stood as it had for unguessed centuries, arrow-straight, its lofty tip far up in the clean reaches of the morning sky. But it seemed to Stagmire as if the giant were shuddering in the throes of some mortal agony. Ripping, crackling sounds, hard as rifle shots, whipped across the slash. The tree was talking all right, crying farewell to the ages of life it had known.

Now it was no longer so proudly erect. That distant tip was moving, swaying into the beginning of a giant arc.

Slowly, grudgingly it moved at first, then with gathering speed. Faster—faster! A wild rushing filled the world, as though some tumultuous wind had suddenly begun to blow. It was a rushing that became a roar, and a roar that peaked up to a thunderous, sudden crash.

The dust of earth and of bark ground to powder spouted up in a cloud, and fragments of splintered branches hurtled out of the pit of chaos along the ridge slope. Then the dust drifted and thinned and settled. A shaken earth steadied, and an awed silence held. The giant was dead, and the skyline lonely with emptiness.

Gaunt and weary as it was, Stagmire's roan horse whirled and fought the reins, snorting in some elemental terror it did not understand. Stagmire, queerly disturbed himself, calmed the animal and looked at the girl again.

Slender and straight she stood, staring at the emptiness of sky that the tree had filled just a few moments before. Her lovely eyes were frankly wet and her soft lips trembling.

The tawny-haired man took her by the arm. "Well, Stewart, now you've seen the boys fell a really big one. Quite a thrill, eh?"

She pulled away from him, brushing a hand

across her eyes, steadying herself. Then she spoke huskily. "No, Ruel . . . not a thrill. A tragedy. I wish I hadn't seen it. It had lived too long to die . . . that way!"

The tawny-haired man laughed. "Nonsense! There's enough good solid lumber in that fellow to build a small community of houses. And that's what our business is, isn't it . . . lumbering?"

The girl did not answer him. Instead, seeming to feel Wade Stagmire's glance, she turned and met it.

"Ma'am," said Stagmire quietly, "I know exactly what you mean."

Once more he touched his hat, then swung the roan away, and rode off down across the slash.

Chapter Two

The headquarters of the Anchor Ranch was log-built and stood on a low bench to the north of the small river that cut down the center of this long-running, timber-rimmed valley. Wade Stagmire, following along the south bank of the river, struck a trail that forded the river at a glinting shallows, crossed over, and came up to the headquarters past a generous spread of split-railed corrals. A sweating, recently run saddle bronco stood ground-reined by the corrals and over on the low porch of the ranch house two men stood, talking.

One of these was a man well past middle age. He was gaunt and grizzled, with fierce and angry eyes. His right leg was twisted and withered and he supported himself on that side with a crutch. The other man was an Indian, stocky, broad, expressionless of face. Both watched Stagmire with an intentness that was wary and suspicious as he rode up and pulled the roan to a tired halt. The voice of the man with the crutch struck out with a harsh rumble.

"Who in hell are you and what do you want?"

"I ate last about forty-eight hours ago," answered Stagmire.

"Damned grubliner, eh?"

This made twice that the name had been thrown

at Stagmire in the past couple of hours, and the contempt wrapped up in it stirred the anger in him. But he kept his tone even and mild.

"Some might call it that and be wrong. I'm flat broke, but I'm no bum. I'll work for what I eat. And I'm damned hungry." Meeting this old fellow's fierce gaze, Stagmire wondered at the strange admixture of emotions reflected in the blazing eyes under the jutting, frosty brows. Rage was there, a bitter, helpless rage, and something almost like despair.

"Where you from?" came the corrosive question.

Stagmire jerked a thumb over his shoulder. "East."

"How far east?"

"Quite a ways. The Sacramento Valley."

The old fellow thought this over, at the same time that his fierce eyes ran up and down Stagmire from head to foot and back again, as though he would take him apart, piece by piece, and see what his complete make-up was.

"Interested in a job . . . a regular job? But a hell of a tough job that could leave you dead out in the timber, or so damn' beat up and broken you couldn't crawl?"

This was shot at him so abruptly, Stagmire for a moment could hardly grasp the implications. Then he was still for a moment, while he considered them.

"It's an honest job," added the old fellow, "if that's the angle that's got you worried."

"We'll talk about it," agreed Stagmire finally.

"Fair enough. What's your name?"

"Stagmire . . . Wade Stagmire."

"I'm Gib Dawson. This is Noyo. He'll feed you. And that roan bronc' of yours looks like it could stand a manger full of hay and a couple of quarts of oats. You'll find both in the barn. Help yourself."

The old fellow spun expertly on his crutch and went into the ranch house. The Indian, Noyo, unsaddled and corralled the horse by the gate, then showed Stagmire where to put the roan and where the oat bin was. After which the Indian went over to the cook shack. Stagmire unsaddled, found an old sack, and gave the roan a good rubdown while the animal munched hungrily.

"I don't know what we've moved into, bronco," murmured Stagmire. "But at least there's a square meal for both of us, which is all that counts right now."

There was a bucket of water and a tin wash basin on a bench by the cook shack door, with a faded towel hanging above. Stagmire treated himself to a wash, then combed his thick brown hair with his fingers. Inside the place a steak was sizzling and the aroma of it set the juices to running in Stagmire's mouth and deepened the hunger in the brightness of his eyes. A strange

17

and shaking weakness ran all through him. This, he thought, was what stark physical need for food could do to a man.

Besides the smoking steak with its oozing, savory richness, Noyo put on the table a big plate of potatoes, half a loaf of bread, and most of a pot of warmed-over coffee. There was also a big wedge of huckleberry pie. Despite his wolfish hunger, Stagmire forced himself to eat slowly, a fact the Indian noted with approval.

"You come long way," said Noyo abruptly.

"Yeah." Stagmire nodded warily. "A long way."

"Where you think you go?"

"Any place . . . no place."

"Mebbe so you stop here," said Noyo. "Mebbe so you go to work for Gib Dawson. Him old . . . got bum leg. Needs a good man in the saddle."

In his dire need for it, these first few mouthfuls of food took hold of Stagmire with all the abruptness a jolt of raw liquor might have given. That strange, gray weakness that had held him, shaken both in mind and body, now softened up and left him. His perspective began to level out. He could think of something else than just food.

"You say Gib Dawson needs a good man in the saddle, Noyo. How do you know I'm a good man?"

Noyo shrugged. "You see a horse. You look at it careful. Then you know if it's a good horse or a bad one."

"Maybe it's not as simple as that," said Stagmire carefully. "Human animals are harder to read than horses. Not so much fundamental honesty in them."

Noyo shrugged again, said nothing more.

Stagmire cleaned up every scrap of food in front of him and finally leaned back with a deep sigh of content, replete as he hadn't been in weeks. Automatically he reached for his smoking, then realized he had none. Seeing the move and understanding, Noyo supplied tobacco and papers. Stagmire spun a cigarette into shape. "That's how flat I am, Noyo. Not even the price of a sack of Durham. Man, you're a damned fine cook. Thanks for everything."

"No thank me," said Noyo. "Thank Gib Dawson." And then he added, with a note of almost fierce intensity: "Him good man, too . . . damn' plenty good!"

Mindful of Gib Dawson's offer, Stagmire left the cook shack and headed over to the ranch house. As he went, he pondered the difference a full stomach could give to a man's outlook on life. An hour ago this had seemed a hostile country, cold and unfriendly. Now there seemed a new warmth to the sun and things were looking up.

Gib Dawson was plainly waiting for him, since as he came up to the ranch house porch, the old cattleman's voice reached out from the open door.

19

"Come on in."

It was bachelor quarters, the furnishings frugal but sufficient and of reasonable comfort. A few chairs, a cluttered table of odds and ends, an old couch along one wall. To the right of the door was a gun rack, holding a couple of Winchester rifles. From one of the pegs hung a worn gun belt and holster and from the holster protruded the butt of a heavy Colt six-shooter.

Gib Dawson sat in an old rocker by an open window, his crutch lying on the floor beside him. His head and shoulders were half in shadow, half in the rays of sunlight glinting through the window. The effect made him look a little old, a little weary, a sort of brooding, helpless weariness. Now, with his deep and shadowed eyes fixed on Stagmire, he said: "Drag up a chair and we'll talk this job proposition over. I hope you're interested."

"That could depend," said Stagmire soberly, "on what you think of me as well as on what I think of you."

"I've done my thinkin'," said Dawson. Then he added dryly: "No future in grublining that I ever heard of."

"What makes you think I could be of any use to you?" asked Stagmire. "You don't know a thing about me."

"I know this much," growled Dawson. "You're new to this country, which means that Frank

Lawrey ain't been able to work on you yet and make a damn' thief out of you. I'll take a chance on all the rest."

Stagmire spoke slowly. "You got to admit that this sounds like desperation on your part. Like you were grabbing at a last and final straw."

"Sure I'm desperate," admitted the old fellow bluntly. "Right now I'd hire anything that could wear pants and straddle a bronc', providing I felt they'd be halfway true to their hire."

"And you think I would?"

"I'm offering you a job, ain't I? Yeah, I'll take a chance."

Now it was Wade Stagmire's turn to study a man more carefully than he had ever done before in his life. Things that had occurred in the not too distant past had filled Stagmire with a vast cynicism concerning men and their integrity. He had become wolf-wary about such things. And so his scrutiny of Gib Dawson was suddenly cold and incisive and merciless. Those deep, somewhat haggard eyes, that seamed, leathery face—how deep did the honor of this old fellow reach? How much trust could be put in him and in his sense of fairness and justice?

Gib Dawson met this sudden hard impact of Stagmire's measuring judgment without the slightest suggestion of wavering or retreat. And then he spoke abruptly and with startling insight.

"Son, somebody's hurt you badly, given you

21

a dirty deal. You've the look about you of a kid that's been whipped for something that wasn't his fault. You needn't worry about me. Even my enemies admit I'm honest . . . maybe too damn' honest."

It was Gib Dawson's show of swift understanding and the tone of his voice that decided Stagmire. He made his decision. He reached in a pocket and brought out a folded paper. It was of cheap, rough stock, tattered about the edges, worn and smudged from carrying. Stagmire unfolded it carefully and held it out.

"After you look this over you'll probably withdraw that offer of a job," he said quietly.

Gib Dawson took the paper, held it where the sun struck it, peered at it long and carefully. Then he swung his head and fixed his fierce old eyes on Stagmire intently.

"Was it?" he demanded harshly.

"Was it what?"

"Murder! That's what it says on this sheriff's dodger. Wade Stagmire . . . wanted for the murder of Dodd Evans!"

Stagmire drew a long breath. "No," he said simply, "it wasn't murder. Oh, I killed him, all right. But it wasn't murder. It wasn't an even break for me. He had two shots at me while my back was turned . . . two shots before I could even turn around or know who was cutting down on me, or why. How he ever missed me,

I'll never know. He was in the mouth of an alley I'd just walked by. But he did miss me. Maybe because it was evening . . . dusk. Maybe because the damned rat didn't even have the nerve to make a clean job of shooting a man in the back. But he tried . . . twice. I caught the flash of his gun on his second shot and that's what I cut loose at. And he dropped. I had a hunch, but I wasn't really rightly certain who it was until I'd walked over to him. So that was how it was, and that's the simple truth."

"But the people in that part of the country," asked Gib Dawson, "how come they wouldn't see it as a straight case of self-defense?"

Stagmire shrugged, bitterness pulling his face into bleakness. "You'd have to know that country and the people in it to understand. You'd have to realize how men can crawl and whine in front of a family that is all-powerful in money and range and politics . . . like the Evans family is. At that I might have been able to make a legitimate self-defense plea stand up if the man I was working for and who I thought was my good friend had stood behind me. But it turned out that *he* just didn't have what it took, and he evidently figured that any mere cowpuncher's neck wasn't worth risking the power and enmity of the Evans family. So there wasn't a thing left for me to do but hide out and then skip the country at the first chance. I collected that dodger off a crossroads signpost

I happened to pass. I took it along so that I could keep reminding myself that it wasn't all a bad dream."

"What set this Dodd Evans after your scalp, son?" asked Dawson.

"We'd never been on very good terms, him and me. We just didn't hit it off. But mainly it started at a dance. There was a waitress, a biscuit shooter from a restaurant in town who Dodd Evans was after. He fancied himself as a ladies' man. Far as I know this waitress was a real nice girl, and she had no use for Dodd Evans at all, which I guess proved that she was smart as well as nice. Anyhow, this night I was dancing with her and Dodd Evans came bulling onto the floor and wanted to cut in, which would have been quite all right if he'd been a regular sort of guy. But I knew the girl didn't want to dance with him, wanted no part of him, so I told him to go peddle his papers. Right away he began getting rough, for he fancied himself that way, too."

Stagmire brooded a moment, then shrugged and went on. "One thing led to another and it wasn't long before me and Evans were out in the street, swapping punches. I gave him a real going over, I guess, and he wasn't man enough to take his licking and like it. A couple of weeks later he laid out for me in that alley. And that's the story."

With measured, even movements, Gib Dawson

tore the dodger to shreds and let the pieces fritter through his fingers.

"Son," he said quietly, "you sling your saddle on the Anchor corral. You and me, we understand each other." The old fellow pushed himself erect, stood balanced on his sound leg, and put out a gnarled hand. "We'll shake on it. I think that today brought me the kind of man I been looking for, for a long, long time. Yeah . . . shake!"

Their hands met and now the conviction swept over Wade Stagmire that here was a man he could believe in and trust to the ends of the earth.

"I'll earn my hire, Mister Dawson . . . and I'll be true to it."

"I know you will, son," was the gruff reply. "And make it plain Gib."

The Indian, Noyo, put his head in at the door. "They come now," he said.

"Hah!" It was at once an exclamation and a savage growl that broke across Gib Dawson's lips. "Three coyotes! Three slimy, crooked, double-crossing thieves! I'd like to hang them. But all I can do is tell them off and fire them. Which I will now do!"

He stooped, caught up his crutch, and stumped out onto the porch. Noyo slipped inside, lifted down one of the Winchester rifles from the rack, and moved to a window. Wade Stagmire, wondering, moved up to the door and looked out.

Three riders were just pulling in at the corrals.

Gib Dawson's voice whipped harshly across at them. "You . . . Trautwine, Krug, Gentry . . . come over here!"

The three stepped from their saddles, stared across at the old cattleman. For a moment they hesitated, some low words passing between them. Then they came on over.

Virg Trautwine was lanky, with a hatchet face. Burt Krug was shorter, thicker through the body, with black curly hair and a round, bland face. Rocky Gentry was of medium size, soft-stepping, a dissipated hardness in his face and eyes. Trautwine seemed to be the spokesman for the three.

"What's on your mind, boss?" he asked with a faint show of truculence. "Me and Burt and Rocky, we've been . . ."

"Never mind the boss stuff," cut in Gib Dawson savagely. "That's all done. And I know where you've been . . . you dirty, damn' crooked whelps! You've been turning over another jag of Anchor cattle to Price Mabry and some others of Frank Lawrey's gang. How much did Mabry pay you this trip?"

Gib Dawson did not give Virg Trautwine a chance to answer, for his harsh fury was deepening and swelling in him. "I've seen some low-down specimens in my time," he went on, raging, "but the lowest of them were upstanding men compared to you three. By rights I should boot you off this ranch without a cent of pay. But I never in all my life held out on any man who ever rode for me, and I'm not starting now. I pay my debts . . . all of them . . . so I pay you. Go get your gear. You're through . . . fired! Come by here when you leave. I'll have your time made out. Hurry up . . . move! You pollute the air and I want to get rid of you!"

Watching, Wade Stagmire saw several expressions pass across the faces of the three. Virg Trautwine began to bluster.

"Dawson, you can't talk to us that way. Why, we don't even know what you're drivin' at! All this talk about us an' cows an' Price Mabry. We . . ."

Gib Dawson waved a weary arm. "Take your damn' lies away with you. Noyo saw what you did. He watched the whole deal. And Noyo don't lie."

Rocky Gentry spat a thin curse. "That damned Indian!" He swung his narrow head, as though looking for Noyo. "Next time I bump into him I'll wear out a quirt on his dumb back. Come on, Virg, Burt! No use tryin' to argue out of it." Gentry turned and headed for the bunkhouse, and the others followed him.

Gib Dawson came back in, his crutch thumping. He sat down at the table and got busy with time and checkbooks. Wade Stagmire stood beside the door, watching and thinking. What he had just heard had set small fires to burning in him. Fidelity to his hire should be an accepted tenet of any rider, as Stagmire saw it. Other misdeeds might be condoned or excused. But when a man turned traitor to his hire, that marked him as about as low as they came. These three had done worse. They were thieves as well as traitors.

"They ready," said Noyo from his window.

Gib Dawson bunched three checks in his hand, went out on the porch again. Burt Krug and Rocky Gentry were in their saddles, while Virg Trautwine came over on foot, leading his horse. There was a sullen look to him. He dropped the reins of his horse and scuffed his spurs truculently as he stepped onto the porch.

"I don't take kindly to the names you been callin' Burt an' Rocky an' me. Watch your tongue, Dawson!"

Gib Dawson held out the checks, looked Trautwine up and down with searing contempt. "You are three damned dirty, thieving whelps," he growled deliberately.

Virg Trautwine took the checks with his left hand and then, with a roll of his shoulder, but no warning, threw his right fist into Gib Dawson's face, snarling thinly: "I warned you, Dawson!"

With only the crutch and one sound leg to hold him up, Gib Dawson was in no condition to take that sudden, cowardly blow. It knocked the old

28

fellow flat, brought the bright crimson of blood to his lips.

Watching from just inside the door, Stagmire could hardly believe his own eyes. That any man would be low and cowardly enough to hit another twice his age, a crippled old fellow with a crutch! A fury that was black and savage surged through Stagmire and his voice rang harshly.

"Watch the other two, Noyo."

Then he went through the door in a long, low lunge that carried him right up to the startled Trautwine. The gangling rider tried to whirl, clawing for his gun. Before he could get it, Stagmire hit him. It was a reaching blow that had all the power of Stagmire's lunge behind it and it made a gory wreck of Trautwine's loose mouth.

Trautwine went reeling, trying desperately to hold his feet. The drop-off of the low porch was only a scant foot, but, when Trautwine's clattering boots struck this emptiness, he went down in a long, tangled sprawl. Stagmire went right after him, kicking the half-drawn gun from Trautwine's hand. Stagmire swung his boot toe again, none too gently.

"Get up!" he gritted. "Get up and take it . . . or I'll kick you all the way to the corrals, the same as I would any other mangy, cowardly whelp. Get up!"

Trautwine managed it, scrambling and floundering. Then Stagmire went to work on him. He belted Trautwine back and forth, cutting him up, punishing him wickedly, hitting hard enough to cut and batter and keep Trautwine off balance and wild, but not hard enough to knock him down again.

Trautwine's few return blows were aimless and wild, doing him little good and Stagmire little harm, for Virg was still numbed from that first stunning smash he had taken. Stagmire swarmed over him, showing him no mercy and feeling none, seeing only Trautwine's battered face through a red mist, and hitting it and hitting it.

Finally, from what seemed a far distance, Stagmire heard Gib Dawson's words. "That's enough, son. Finish it!"

So Stagmire set himself, straightened Trautwine with a crackling left, and then uncoiled all the way from his heels behind a final blasting right fist. The blow spun Trautwine completely around and dropped him in a quivering heap.

Stagmire backed up a couple of steps, felt his boot heel hit a hard object. It was Trautwine's gun. Stagmire caught it up, and in a slightly crouched prowl headed for Burt Krug and Rocky Gentry who were still in their saddles, set and staring. Stagmire's words lashed out, hoarse with feeling.

"Now then, maybe you two rats would like to make a real fight of this? If you feel that way, get to it!"

Krug and Gentry made no move, and for several reasons. One was that the stocky figure of Noyo stood in the ranch house door, a rifle across his arm. Another was that they'd just seen Virg Trautwine, supposedly a pretty fair man with his fists, whipped to a bleeding rag in a brief thirty seconds by this ragged, cold-jawed stranger now challenging them. They wanted no part of anything, just now.

Gib Dawson's grim voice reached out again. "Tell them to put Trautwine across his saddle and get him out of here."

Stagmire gave Virg Trautwine's gun a little wave. "You heard. Get about it!"

Krug and Gentry dismounted and went over to Trautwine. They propped him up, got him to his feet, and half carried him to his horse. Virg's head was sagging and he was only partially conscious. Grunting and cursing, they boosted him into his saddle. The checks Virg had held were scattered on the earth. Stagmire picked them up, pushed them at Krug.

"That'll be all."

The three of them rode away, downslope toward the river. Gentry and Krug had to ride on either side of Virg, steadying him in the saddle. When the tangle of alders along the stream hid them, Wade Stagmire turned and went slowly back to the ranch house porch.

Gib Dawson was on his feet again, his crutch

31

under his arm. With his shirt sleeve he'd wiped the blood from his mouth. Now he was staring bleakly across the sunlit little valley, and the look on his face made Wade Stagmire wince. For he knew what Gib Dawson was thinking.

The grizzled cattleman was looking back at the years when he'd been a whole man and a younger one, back to days when no surly cowhand would have dared lift a hand against him—back to days when he'd been able to fight his own battles and hold his own against any man. While now . . .

There was a singularly deep and hurting tragedy in this moment, and Wade Stagmire respected it by keeping complete silence, while his own thoughts went back to an earlier moment of this day when he'd seen the great redwood tree fall. Somehow there was a similarity in these things. That great tree—this grizzled old-timer, Gib Dawson . . . The cattleman shook himself, turned toward the ranch house door. "Thanks, son," he said gruffly. "Now come on in here. We got things to talk about."

Noyo had put the rifle back on the rack. He stood at the side of the door when Stagmire entered. He dropped a hand on Stagmire's arm with a quick, firm pressure and in the Indian's black eyes there was a deep and shining light. "I said it," murmured Noyo. "Good man."

Chapter Three

Gib Dawson sat in the old rocker by the window, packing a stubby pipe with tobacco. He lit up, lipping the pipe stem gingerly because of his cut mouth. Presently he spoke.

"You just saw a small part, a very small part of the situation, son. Still interested in that job?"

"We settled that a little while ago," Stagmire answered quietly. "I'm with you as long as you want me."

The old rocker creaked gently and smoke wreathed Gib Dawson's face. "That river down yonder . . . it's the Sotoyome . . . flows into the Pacific Ocean about ten miles from here. On a headland above the mouth of the river is Castle City. Mainly it's a lumbering town. You might say that Jared Hubbard owns that town, same as he owns the big sawmill there. Besides that, he's got a bunch of logging camps back in the redwoods. He's got plenty of loggers and mill hands to feed, so he uses a lot of beef.

"Frank Lawrey's got a contract with Hubbard to furnish that beef. Some of it he raises on his Wagon Wheel Ranch about twenty miles down the coast. Some of it he brings down from Eureka, or even up from San Francisco by boat. And some of it he rustles from me, which is the angle we're interested in. I ain't the only one that Lawrey's had his gang of tough riders work on. I could name you three or four other outfits that used to run cattle on the various inland valley ranges and went busted because Lawrey stole all their profits away. And he'll have me in the same spot in another six months or less, unless I can put a crimp in him some way."

"This fellow Hubbard," said Stagmire. "Doesn't he know he's buying rustled beef? Have you ever tried appealing to him? From what you say of him he must be a pretty big man and men that size don't get that way by conniving with some damned cow thief."

A grim and mirthless smile touched Gib Dawson's face. "You'd have to meet Jared Hubbard and get to know him a little to get a better answer to that than I can give you, son. He's a big man, all right . . . in his own opinion an awful big man. Almost as big as God Almighty. He's gotten rich and getting richer by the minute. He owns an empire and he's an emperor, you might say. He sits in his office and listens to the saws in the mill whining out more dollars for him at every pass. Understand, I'm not saying he's in any way crooked. Far as I know, he's honest enough. But it's just that he's a mite blinded by his own importance and just can't be bothered by the affairs of a little guy like me. Just so long as his empire keeps running smooth, that's good enough for Jared Hubbard."

Dawson paused to freshen his pipe with another match, puffing furiously for a moment before going on.

"The fellow who knows all about how Frank Lawrey gets a lot of his beef is Ruel Tedrow, Hubbard's general superintendent. Tedrow is Hubbard's right-hand man and Hubbard leaves all the details like supplying the cook houses and boarding houses for the logging crews and mill hands strictly up to him. The cheaper Tedrow can run those places while still keeping the loggers and mill hands happy and satisfied with their grub, the better the books look to Jared Hubbard. So, when Tedrow buys beef, the cheaper he can get it, the better, and to hell with where it comes from. Naturally Frank Lawrey can sell rustled beef plenty cheap and still make a profit. So now you have the general picture, and I agree with you that it ain't a very promising one from where we stand."

Wade Stagmire took a turn or two up and down the room. There was, he realized grimly, no question about his needing a job and needing it badly. He didn't have a dime in his jeans, not even smoking money. His gun—well, he'd had to sell that to eat, along his getaway trail. And to get the meal he'd just eaten a little while ago, he'd had to grubline, a practice that would never set well with a man of pride. And Stagmire had his good share of this.

But the job he was taking on now with Gib Dawson was little short of fantastic. He, a total stranger in a strange land, trying to take hold and get results against such a set-up as Gib Dawson had just outlined—fantastic, indeed.

He stopped beside Gib Dawson's chair, looked down at the old fellow. "I'm taking the job, of course. But what good I can do you, if any, I'm no ways sure. I'm afraid you see me as a damned sight bigger man than I see myself, Gib."

The cattleman grunted. "You've growed a heap since I first set eyes on you, son. You measure pretty damn' tall and wide."

"This fellow, Tedrow," said Stagmire thoughtfully. "A big man, heavy-shouldered, florid-faced, and with a shock of yellow hair?"

Gib Dawson swung his head in some surprise. "That's him! You've met him?"

"Yeah." Stagmire nodded, telling of the meeting up in the slash where the big redwood tree had been felled. "Lot of arrogance in that fellow," he ended.

"Arrogant and crooked!" snorted Gib Dawson. "Just as crooked as Frank Lawrey. And cruel. Another man's neck don't mean a damn' thing to Ruel Tedrow. He's stepped on plenty of them, getting up to where he is. But Jared Hubbard swears by him, blinded maybe by the fact that

Tedrow gets things done for him. Why, I've even heard it said that Hubbard would like nothing better than to see Tedrow marry his niece, once she gets back from the East where she's been getting a heap of schooling. And that would sure be pure hell for that girl, for no sweeter, finer girl ever lived than Stewart Hubbard. I knew that youngster well. Before Hubbard sent her East to school she used to ride out here and visit with me, regular. Had a little Indian paint pony and I tell you it was mighty fine to see her come riding up from the river, pretty as a spring morning, coming to spend the day with old Gib Dawson. Me, I'm hoping Stewart meets up with some fine young feller in the East and marries him and to hell with what Jared Hubbard thinks."

"There was a girl with Ruel Tedrow this morning," said Wade Stagmire. "Pretty . . . like you say. Just about the prettiest girl I ever saw. Black hair, big gray eyes . . ."

"Lord Almighty!" burst out Dawson, rearing forward in his chair. "That's Stewart."

"I heard Tedrow call her by that name," Stagmire agreed. "She was the one who gave me directions to this ranch."

"That's Stewart," said Dawson again. "So she's back. Wonder if she's forgotten me? I sure would like to see that girl again." The old fellow lay back in his chair, his fierce eyes softening over past memories.

37

Stagmire took another turn along the room. "Those three you fired today, Gib . . . they were all the crew you had?"

"They were all." The cattleman cleared his throat harshly. "Once there were three others. I let them go, damn' fool that I was. I believed lies about them that Virg Trautwine told me. But now I know they were good men, while it was Trautwine himself along with Krug and Gentry who were crooked. Yeah, Bill Vessels and Buck Hare and Harley Jacks were damn' good men. I can see that now. But then I was too damn' blind and stupid to realize it. I sure wish I had them back with me."

"Where are they now?"

"Not rightly sure. I did hear that Harley Jacks and Buck Hare were talking of starting up a little spread of their own in Wind Pike Valley. That's north of here about ten miles. Maybe Bill Vessels went in with them. Or maybe they never did get an outfit going. With this bum leg I don't get around much any more. All I know I got to depend on others to tell me and so much of the time it's just talk and nothing else."

"Well," said Stagmire, "one thing is damned certain. We got to scare up some riders somewhere. Looking over the picture you've painted, it's certain that Noyo and I can't handle it all. Do you think there'd be any chance of me picking up some extra hands in this Castle City, was I to ride out there?"

"You might," conceded Dawson. "Worth trying, anyhow. Like I said, Castle City is a lumbering town. But some stray riders drift in and out from time to time. Between here and Eureka there's quite a few cattle layouts, back in the inland valleys. And you know how cowhands come and go. Yeah, you might find what we want in Castle City."

"Then I'll give it a try," declared Stagmire. "Today. And if I can't locate any there, why then I'll take a trip north and inland and see what I can do."

Gib Dawson got up, went over to the table, and reached for his checkbook. He scribbled for a moment, then tore out the check, and handed it to Stagmire.

"You got to have some money in your jeans, son. Call this an advance against your wages. If you don't mind my saying so, you could use a new pair of jeans and a new shirt. You can cash this at Sam Alexander's store in Castle City."

Wade Stagmire glanced at the check, folded it, and stowed it carefully away. He spoke a little huskily. "You sure are showing a lot of trust in a man on the dodge and wanted for murder, Gib."

"Murder be damned," growled Dawson. "That word never did fit you and never will." He stumped over to the gun rack and lifted down the belt and holstered Colt gun that hung there. "Mine," he said. "And an honest outfit. Yours, now. Strap it on, son. After what you did to Virg Trautwine, the word will spread. And there's Krug and Gentry, who might get ideas. If they do, pin their ears back. And understand this. I'll stand with you through hellfire. I'll back your hand to the last jump. That's a promise."

Stagmire strapped on the gun. Gib Dawson followed him to the door. "You'll hit the town trail along the north bank of the river, just below the ford. Ketch yourself up a fresh bronc'. That roan of yours has earned a rest. And, son . . . though it shapes up as a damn' tough fight ahead, I got a feeling about it. I think my luck's changed. And yours."

Chapter Four

Dressed in new, clean clothes, from the skin out, shaven and shorn, Wade Stagmire stepped from the door of a barbershop. He had cashed the check Gib Dawson had given him at Sam Alexander's big general store, made his clothes purchases along with several other minor items, then sought out this barbershop and, in addition to a shave and haircut, had bought himself a steaming, luxurious bath, out back. The all-over change gave him the feeling of being almost newly born. Now he was ready to start earning some part of that advance in wages.

This main street of Castle City ran north and south, with several lesser streets cutting across at right angles. The buildings were virtually all of redwood lumber, solidly built, with board sidewalks scarred and splintered from the calked boots of loggers. There were a number of these in evidence, burly fellows, in Mackinaws or cruiser shirts and stagged trousers, their boots crunching as they swaggered along.

Jared Hubbard's sawmill lay southwest of town, along the curve of the headland where the long, lower lagoon of the Sotoyome River flowed into a sizable cove that was rimmed with low cliffs and studded with black, dripping rocks, around and over which the surf boiled and creamed endlessly. Beyond the cove was the ocean itself, gray-green, surging, never still, and vast as the world was vast. The breath of it was gusty and full of salty vigor and its voice was solid and constant and elemental as the great combers swelled and rolled and crashed their might against the outer headland.

Mighty as the ocean's roar was, it could not smother the song of the saws in Jared Hubbard's mill. Hungry saws, droning sleepily one moment, but in the next setting up a high, penetrating, savage whine as they bit into still another log. There were a hundred lesser noises, but these were the two that dominated all else, the ocean's rumble and the metallic scream of the saws.

Wade Stagmire had never seen the ocean before, so his first move on reaching Castle City, before doing anything else, had been to ride around the northern end of town, out to a point of the headland, and from there have his good look at the might and sweep of the sea, while savoring its penetrating, vigorous breath.

This was a thing he had promised himself when he made his getaway from the threat that hovered over him in the Sacramento Valley; with luck he would ride west until he met the ocean's shore. Which was just about as far as a man in the saddle might flee an unjust charge and the hate of a vengeful Evans clan. Here, in this far and comparatively isolated country, a man might lose himself and gain a new start in life. . . .

The barbering, the bath, the lift of respect given by new clothes brought out the comparative youth in Stagmire, accented the tough leanness in him, deepened the cool gleam in his eye, and put a new and confident spring in his stride. At this moment he carried his good years lightly and confidently.

This town had been built by lumber and because of lumber, but Stagmire found that his dress of a saddle man and the gun at his hip occasioned no undue interest on the part of other men as he passed along the street. This redwood coast was wild country and men of all sorts and callings moved along its trails and through its towns, and their business was accepted as their own. Stagmire, in search of other men of his calling, had no idea where such might be found and for a time was at a loss. Finally, along a side street, he saw several saddle mounts scattered along a hitch rail in front of a saloon with a weathered sign that read simply: CATTLEMAN.

He pushed open the swinging doors and stepped into the place and was instantly struck and alerted by the impact of a harsh and reckless voice delineating the doubtful antecedents and ancestors of someone in no uncertain terms. He paused and listened, while blinking his eyes to adjust them to the change of light.

A big, raw-boned man, with craggy features and a bristly ruff of iron-gray hair showing beneath his pushed-back Stetson, was having his say. He had his back to the bar, his elbows resting on the top of it, and with a boot heel hooked over the brass foot rail. He looked completely relaxed, but the cold shine in his frosty eyes was a measure of his alertness. His voice had a ring to it.

"I say again that you two, along with Virg Trautwine, make up three of the most unlovely lice I ever met up with. You're all crooked drunken snakes and there's not a smidgen of truth in the whole stinking passel of you. Now you know, and if you don't like it, what are you going to do about it?"

This was fighting talk in any man's language, thrown deliberately and contemptuously.

The two riders facing the speaker were drawn a little apart, in effect cornering this bold speaker against the bar. Other men, with one exception, had drawn away, pushing well back to the far corners of the room, giving the central three plenty of leeway. The atmosphere of the place was taut and explosive.

The other lone individual who had remained at the bar was some fifteen feet along toward the far end. He had a whiskey bottle and a glass in front of him, but was making no move toward pouring himself a drink just now. Instead, he was watching the central trio with intent, sardonic eyes.

He was a long-bodied man, lank about the middle, and his stringy hair, hanging ragged at his shirt collar, was coarse and rusty-looking. He had a narrow face with a small, hooked nose and a tight slit of a mouth. A heavy gun sagged at his right hip.

Stagmire, his eyes now mastering the half light of this place, took in all these factors with a swift, flickering survey.

He saw more. He saw that the two riders facing the reckless speaker at the bar were no other than Burt Krug and Rocky Gentry. And, though they were two to one and had their man virtually between them, they were plainly reluctant to force the issue.

The lank, pale-eyed rider farther along the bar cursed in a sudden thin contempt.

"What the hell's the matter with you two? If you expect to ride with me, you got to show more spine than this. I wouldn't let God Almighty, let alone Bill Vessels, talk to me that way . . . and take it."

Bill Vessels! The name hit sharply at Stagmire. This big, raw-boned, reckless fellow was a man who had once ridden for Gib Dawson, and who Dawson was wishing wistfully were back on the Anchor payroll.

Now Bill Vessels pushed a little forward from

the bar, turning slightly so that he might watch not only the two in front of him, but also the lank and pale-eyed speaker. But his returning words ran just as rough and reckless as before.

"Everything I said about these two goes double for you, Mabry. What are you so damned proud about? You steal 'em for Lawrey and Lawrey sells 'em to Tedrow. You're all in the same litter, all in the same basket of snakes!"

A hushed sigh ran over the room. Men crowded back a little farther. The lank one with the pale and strangely cruel eyes backed away from the bar two long and careful steps.

"Well, now," he droned. "We'll see about this!"

Everything was in the fire now. The pot was boiling savagely and about to run over. Every man in the place knew it, and none more surely than this man, Bill Vessels. Watching him, Wade Stagmire saw that Bill Vessels had no illusions concerning the odds now facing him—impossible odds. Yet it was characteristic of this reckless, harsh-voiced fellow that, having made his say, he was ready to back it up, to make the deadly ride, come what would. Here might have been faulty judgment, but here also was bleak, unyielding courage.

It was strictly none of Stagmire's business, yet that man yonder was Bill Vessels, a good man, according to Gib Dawson. Certainly too good, thought Stagmire, to go into this thing alone. So now, through this one long moment of suspended silence that filled the room with an almost intolerable strain, Stagmire's voice drifted, soft, yet penetrating. "Let's keep this thing reasonably even. Three to one is just too damned stiff to swallow. Cut it fine, mister . . . cut it fine!"

The lank one—Price Mabry—went very still. He seemed to hold his breath for a moment, then let it out in a faint, sibilant hiss. His narrow head came slowly around, but he made no other move. Stagmire watched him unwinkingly.

"Yeah," murmured Stagmire. "It's you I mean . . . you!"

Price Mabry had a reputation along this wild coast country. It wasn't any kind of reputation to be proud of, but it was one that most men were careful to walk around. Price Mabry was no coward. There was a black, perverted pride in the man that would not let him be that—at least not publicly. Privately there was no telling, for what went on deep within the dark recesses of this man's mind and soul, no other man could ever guess.

Yet, when it came to gun play, Mabry was coldly realistic. He knew his own capabilities in such matters and had his own confidence in them. But it had been a lifelong rule of his never to test like capabilities in another man until he'd had a chance to study that man and arrive at a satisfactory estimate. Neither did Price Mabry ever refuse to maneuver for some possible edge of advantage when a smoke rolling was imminent.

For one short breath, that edge had been his in this affair. Now it was gone, in fact stood against him. And to him, Wade Stagmire was a complete stranger, a man he'd never laid eyes on before. And the unknown, as Price Mabry well knew, could be highly dangerous. Particularly where violence and gun play were concerned.

This thing had gone sour. The physical set-up was all wrong. The unknown was at his back. If Mabry wanted to force the issue now, he'd have to turn to shoot. Wade Stagmire didn't have to turn. That made the big difference, the difference between living and dying. So Price Mabry, swiftly weighing all these factors in the shadowy depths of his mind, stepped back to the bar, poured himself a drink, and downed it.

Wade Stagmire moved up beside him, on his right side and just a trifle to the rear, smart enough to hold this advantage. He threw a swift glance along the bar, met Bill Vessels's wondering, but frankly relieved eyes.

"Now, friend," said Stagmire, "you can clear the air."

Bill Vessels knew the answer to this. The big fellow put all his attention on Burt Krug and Rocky Gentry. "Git!" he ordered harshly. "Light a shuck! You might have had ideas a couple of minutes ago, but you've changed them by now. I know it and you know it. Git!"

They didn't argue. At Wade Stagmire's first words they had, like Price Mabry, swung startled heads and found themselves looking at the same man who had taken Virg Trautwine apart out at Anchor headquarters. They had sensed the unknown, just as Price Mabry had, and had seen just enough of it to want no further part of it, not at this time, at least. They turned, shuffled to the door, and went out.

Bill Vessels followed them to the door, held it partly open, watched for a moment to make sure the two were really on their way. Then he came back to the bar and dropped in on the left side of Price Mabry.

"Now then, Mabry," he drawled, "what was it you were saying?"

Price Mabry gave no answer. He poured himself another drink, took a coin from his pocket, spun it along the bar. Then he backed away, keeping his hands strictly neutral. He spoke, and his voice held that same thin drone.

"Hell with you, Vessels!" His pale, cruel glance ran up and down Wade Stagmire, measuring, storing things away in his dark mind. "If you stay in these parts, mister . . . there'll come another time. Then . . . we'll see."

He turned and went out, spur rowels scuffing.

The room seemed to brighten. Men's voices,

held silent before, now struck up a quick chattering, a trifle high-pitched from bottled-up strain. Some moved to the bar, others back to interrupted card games. The bartender, a short, paunchy man with thinning hair, wiped his face with the tail of his apron, clattered bottles and glasses noisily.

"Bill," he said to Vessels, "only a reckless damn' fool like you would spit in the devil's eye. Man! You had me scared!"

Vessels showed a hard grin. "Had myself scared, Obie. But the day I walk around Price Mabry, or such lice as Krug and Gentry, why that day I ain't fit to live any longer. Yet you're right, of course. I sure had my neck out that time."

He turned and faced Wade Stagmire fully. "I don't know why you did it, friend . . . but you sure did. I'd let myself in for something, and the squeeze was on. Your prying Mabry off my back was a gift from heaven I sure didn't expect. Now get this. Everything I said about Price Mabry being a damned thief is true enough. But I want to add now that he's bad medicine any way you take him, particularly with a gun. Which I'm hoping you'll remember. Keep your eye on that jigger. Which leaves me trying to say thanks. I'd like to buy you a drink. What'll you have? Me . . . I'm Bill Vessels."

"Stagmire here, Wade Stagmire. Glad to know

you, Vessels. Gib Dawson was telling me about you."

"Gib Dawson! You know him?"

"Riding for him." Stagmire nodded.

"The devil! I can't figure that. Those two . . . Krug and Gentry, they're Anchor hands. How come you didn't . . . ?"

"They *were* Anchor hands," cut in Stagmire, smiling briefly. "They and a fellow named Trautwine. Gib Dawson fired all of them today."

"Well," grunted Vessels, "that's news. I thought Dawson figgered them as three fair-haired boys. How come he gave them their time?"

"Found out they were selling him out to a guy named Frank Lawrey."

"Hah! So the old fool finally woke up, did he? Me and a couple of other boys tried to wise him up to those three rats some time ago. But he wouldn't listen to us. Serves him right."

Wade Stagmire poured himself a short drink. He lifted the glass, stared at it, spinning the liquor in it. He spoke softly.

"Gib Dawson is a mighty fine man. But being tied down like he is with a bad leg, unable to get around and see to his own interests personally, having to leave all that sort of thing up to hired hands, and being worked on all the time the way he has been by this fellow Frank Lawrey, well, Gib Dawson can be excused a few mistakes in judgment. I wonder, Vessels, if you or I were

51

in Dawson's boots, whether we wouldn't make worse ones?"

Vessels downed his drink. "You're driving at something, friend. What?"

Stagmire spun a cigarette into shape, picking his words carefully.

"Gib Dawson told me about how he happened to let you go, you and a couple of other riders by name of Harley Jacks and Buck Hare. He said he'd realized long since that he'd made a bad mistake there, admitting that you were three damned good men. And he wishes he had you back, all of you, riding for him."

Bill Vessels accepted tobacco and papers from Stagmire, built a smoke for himself. "The darned old fool," he growled. "I liked Gib Dawson . . . liked him a heap. Still do, I reckon. But when a man you've ridden for and given your best to turns on you and brands you as crooked . . . and gives you your time on that angle . . . well . . ." Vessels's growl ran out and he shrugged.

"An old man, tied down with a crippled leg. Being pushed around and robbed at every turn of the trail," reminded Stagmire. "Yet a damned good man and one not afraid to admit he'd been wrong."

Bill Vessels swung his head, laid an intent glance on Stagmire. "Maybe he sent you to town to try and locate me or Harley or Buck and get us to come back and sign on again with Anchor?"

52

"That's right, he did," admitted Stagmire, his eyes smiling back at Vessels.

"Then maybe that's why you stepped in on that threatened ruckus, siding me against those three? You heard Price Mabry name me. Maybe you figgered then that out of gratitude I'd . . . ?"

"No. Not for that reason. Maybe I just liked the damned fool reckless way you threw it back at that crowd. And . . . well, it was three to one . . ." Stagmire shrugged.

Bill Vessels stared thoughtfully at the backbar mirror. "When Gib Dawson let us go, Harley and Buck and me, we figgered to put in together and start a little spread of our own in Wind Pike Valley. It's been tough sledding. We got a few cows together and they were ours, up to three days ago. They're gone, now."

Vessels paused, inhaled deeply, blew thin smoke through pursed lips. "Me and Harley and Buck, we were on the upper end of our range, fencing in some springs. It was a two-day job and a good fifteen miles from headquarters. Rather than make the ride back and forth for grub and a bed, we camped overnight on the job. That was a mistake on our part. Lawrey must have had somebody spying on us. Anyhow, while we were away those two days, they cleaned every damned head of our cattle off our lower range, where our cows happened to be running at the time. So now we got a range but no cattle . . . and no money."

Vessels poured himself another drink, his face moody.

"You name this fellow Lawrey as responsible," said Stagmire. "You're sure of that?"

Vessels jerked his head emphatically. "Plumb. He's the only one in these parts who could pull a steal like that and get away with it. He's got the men, the means, and a market handy for the beef."

"Selling to Hubbard, you mean?"

"Not direct to Hubbard. But to Ruel Tedrow, who does the buying for Hubbard's logging camps and mill boarding houses. Which amounts to the same thing."

"How many head did you and your partners lose?"

"About eighty head. Not much of a herd by some standards, mebbe. But it was a fair start that we figgered to build on. Every thin dime we had in the world was tied up in the cattle. So now," ended Vessels, with a wry grimace, "me and Harley and Buck are three very down-and-out saddle pounders, all done with dreaming, and back to the hard realities of a damned tough world."

"There's a job waiting for all three of you out at Anchor, if you're interested," said Stagmire. "I hope you are."

"What good would that do us?" brooded Vessels. "Gib Dawson can't last. He's getting

54

near the end of his string. Time Frank Lawrey gets through with him, he won't be any better off than me and Harley and Buck."

"If Gib Dawson goes down," said Stagmire with slow emphasis, "*if* he does, then he'll go down fighting. And me and one damned good Indian, Noyo, we'll go down with him. But before that happens, somebody will know they've been in one wild old waltz. You can bet your shirt on that."

"I like your spirit, but can't say much for your judgment," observed Vessels dryly. "You can't fight Frank Lawrey and him with the backing of Ruel Tedrow, which means the backing of Jared Hubbard. Too much money . . . too much power, there. Frank Lawrey will end up owning every decent piece of range in fifty miles along this coast. After he busts everybody else, that range will be his for the taking."

"All the range a dead man owns," said Stagmire, a new and cold note coming into his voice, "is a piece six feet long and three feet wide. Could be that this Frank Lawrey will find that out."

Again Bill Vessels put his glance intently on Stagmire. "You really mean to go after Lawrey, don't you?"

"That's right. I ride this thing through with Gib Dawson, regardless. I wish you were riding with us, Bill."

Vessels stared down, slid a foot back and forth along the boot rail. Finally his head came up. "Mebbe I'm a damned fool, but you got a look about you that I like, friend. I'll talk things over with Harley and Buck. I ain't promising a thing, understand. But it could be that you'll be seeing us, out at Anchor."

"We'll drink on that hope," said Stagmire quickly. "And I'll buy this one, Bill."

They drank, looked at each other, and then, moved by a common impulse, shook hands.

Vessels grinned crookedly. "You could sell spectacles to a blind Indian, fellah. Tell Gib Dawson to break out the fatted calf. And here's something I said once before, but I'll say it again. You watch yourself. You made Price Mabry take water today. He ain't ever going to forget that, so don't you forget it, either. For Price Mabry is a plumb bad one, bad from any angle you see him."

Chapter Five

Jared Hubbard was a slender, precise man, with neatly trimmed iron-gray hair and addicted to well-tailored gray suits and starched and immaculate linen. His features were fine-boned, well and evenly cut. He would have been a very handsome man if his rather colorless face had reflected more of geniality and less of severity and a pride that would not let him unbend.

His life was the big lumber concern of which he was the absolute head. His passion was for the efficient functioning of that concern and the solid handling of the profits his efficient functioning built up. His one weakness and real extravagance was his niece, Stewart. Nothing was too good for her. There were those, however, who vowed that this concern for the girl's welfare was due more to Jared Hubbard's burning desire to assure that the future of the Hubbard lumber empire should remain forever in the Hubbard family, than because of any real fondness for the girl herself.

This talk was unjust to Jared Hubbard. While he did hope and plan for the furtherance of Hubbard interests in Hubbard hands, Jared Hubbard's affection for his niece was very real and very deep. A widower of many years' standing, and childless, there was more of his finer interests in life tied up in Stewart than even he himself realized. Yet, because of the driving ambitions that had carried him all his life and because both he and the girl were dominant personalities in their respective rights, they clashed often on various matters of import.

On this clear and sunny afternoon, the two of them were alone in Jared Hubbard's big and expensively appointed office. This was in the second story of a building, so situated that from its windows Jared Hubbard could look out and across the drying yards to the big mill, a scene throbbing and humming with activity.

Sometimes Hubbard would sit for hours, just looking at this enterprise he had fashioned. On this day his niece was standing at a window, looking out, not at the mill or drying yard, but beyond all this to the far and shining sea. Her slim shoulders were very erect and there was the faint shadow of impatience and discomfort in her wide, gray eyes. She spoke without turning.

"Please understand, Uncle Jared, that I fully appreciate all the kindnesses you have shown me, all the things you have done for me. I don't want you to think me ungrateful, but I'm definitely not interested in any thought of marriage, and I will not be until the right man comes along."

Jared Hubbard stood beyond the desk, his hands clasped behind him. "There are," he said, with his usual precise manner, "more things to be considered about a sound and thoughtful marriage than the mere question of love, Stewart. There are certain responsibilities one owes to his or her name and family. As you grow older you will realize that. Now then, you are fully aware of my strong desire to see the Hubbard interests carried on within the family. I have long since seen to it that when I am gone, everything I own will go to you. But while I do not underestimate your clear-headedness and common sense . . . and yes, your business acumen, I can't help but feel that the proper management of Hubbard affairs might be a little beyond you. I feel that perhaps you would need the help of a man trained in the organization and capable of not only holding the business together, but also of expanding and strengthening it. There is such a man."

Stewart turned and faced him. "You're referring to Ruel Tedrow, of course," she said quietly. "I like Ruel, Uncle Jared. But I am very far from being in love with him, and I'll never marry a man I do not love. Perhaps my ideas in such things are old-fashioned, but, as I see it, any marriage not based on love primarily, regardless of its material advantages, would be mockery of the worst sort."

"I'm merely trying to be logical, Stewart," persisted Jared Hubbard. "And . . ."

"Logical, perhaps," cut in Stewart, "but don't

you realize that a woman's heart and mind are notorious for being illogical?" She showed him a small, affectionate smile. "You're floundering in depths you do not understand, Uncle Jared. Now what do you say that we drop the subject, please?"

Stewart turned back to the window again and Jared Hubbard stared at her uncompromising back. In some ways the years of schooling in the East had changed this niece of his a great deal, but in others, not at all. The strong streak of independent thought that she had shown back when she was just a long-legged, harum-scarum youngster, galloping her pinto pony along some foaming, spume-sprinkled beach, black hair flying in the wind, eyes sparkling and cheeks glowing with the sheer joy of living, was still in her. Even as a child she could be led, but never driven, and in these things, Jared Hubbard reflected, the human spirit never changed.

"There is, of course," he meditated, "no immediate rush in this matter, and I did not intend to convey the idea that there was. But I do want you to think over your responsibilities, Stewart, and be guided by the convictions you're bound to arrive at."

Her reply was quiet but firm. "My sense of responsibilities, Uncle Jared, will never outweigh the wisdom of my heart. I'm not at all certain that I like the lumbering industry at all. This morning I rode out with Ruel Tedrow to see some loggers fell a really big redwood. It was a patriarch among trees, something that had been growing and thriving for hundreds, perhaps a thousand years. Now it is gone, and I can't forget how empty the sky looked after the felling."

Jared Hubbard laughed in sheer disbelief. "Child, you can't be serious. Why, the needs of men . . ."

She turned and stopped him with a wave of her hand.

"I know. I've heard all that before, Uncle Jared. Ruel lectured me all the way back to town in that same vein. Maybe such things are necessary. No doubt they are. But I don't have to like them. As it stood, the tree was magnificent, majestic. Felled and sawn up into lumber, well . . . there'll merely be some more houses, growing swiftly tawdry because tawdry people will live in them. I'm afraid," she ended, "that I'm a great disappointment to you, Uncle Jared."

Before he could answer this, the door of the office opened and Hubbard's secretary, a mousy, thin-faced little woman, slipped in.

"Please excuse me, Mister Hubbard, but there is a man in the outer office who insists on seeing you. A Mister Stagmire . . . a cowboy. He is a very determined young man. I told him you were too busy to see him, but that doesn't budge him. What shall I do with him?"

Stewart was plainly relieved at the interruption

61

and she spoke quickly. "I'm sure Uncle Jared isn't too busy now, Miss Murdock. He and I have had our talk."

Jared Hubbard's face tightened and there was some anger in his stride as he stamped up to his desk. "Stagmire," he snapped. "A cowboy. I never heard of him before and what business would I have with him? But . . . show him in!"

If Wade Stagmire was in any way awed or impressed by the elegance of Jared Hubbard's office, he did not show it. He had left his spurs hanging on the horn of his saddle and so now his step was the light, sure one of a man perfectly co-ordinated. He did know some surprise at sight of the girl who had given him directions to Gib Dawson's ranch. He had his hat in his hand, so now he tipped his head slightly and gravely toward her, before facing Jared Hubbard, who was looking at him with no friendliness at all. Hubbard spoke curtly.

"I can imagine no reason at all for this call, Mister Stagmire. I deal in lumber, not cattle."

"I'm not so sure of that Mister Hubbard," said Stagmire quietly. "Particularly stolen cattle."

Jared Hubbard gave the appearance of one who could hardly believe his own ears. "Stolen cattle! I'm afraid I don't understand you, sir. What conceivable interest would I have in stolen cattle? I say again, this is the office of a lumbering industry."

"The stolen cattle, Mister Hubbard, end up as beef on the tables of your logging camps and mill-hand boarding houses. A lot of Gib Dawson's cattle have ended up there, and I'm asking you to put a stop to that sort of business."

Jared Hubbard laughed in disbelief. "Mister Stagmire, are you joking? If so, I don't like the sound of it and wish to hear no more of it."

Wade Stagmire shook his head, his glance holding cool and direct. "Far from a joke. Anchor cattle have been and are being stolen by one Frank Lawrey, who slaughters the critters and then sells the beef to your company through a man named Ruel Tedrow. It's your money that buys the beef, Mister Hubbard, and therefore you are certainly in a position to put a stop to it."

The momentary bewilderment in Jared Hubbard's eyes was replaced by the glint of a very real anger. "Sir, this is preposterous and I resent your statement. By direct implication you are accusing my general superintendent, Mister Tedrow, of dishonest dealings, and dragging me into it, also. Let me tell you that Ruel Tedrow is a thoroughly reliable man in whom I repose the greatest confidence. Let me tell you also that the Hubbard logging and lumbering organization does not, or does not need to, deal in anything off-color or in any way unsavory. I say again that I resent your statements and I resent your presence in this office. You will kindly leave!"

Stagmire did not move. "Then you refuse to look into the matter and put a stop to it, Mister Hubbard?"

"I refuse to believe you even know what you're talking about, sir," snapped Jared Hubbard. "Miss Murdock will show you out."

Stagmire shrugged. "Sorry you feel this way. I was told you were a fair man and I came to you fairly. But if you refuse to do anything in this affair, then Anchor is going to have to. And it may get . . . rough."

Hubbard stiffened. "Are you trying to threaten me? You'd dare . . . in my own office?"

"No, Mister Hubbard. Not threatening you or anyone else. Just stating a few facts and asking for a square deal."

Stagmire turned to leave, his glance touching the girl by the window, who was watching him, wide and sober of eye. Just a glimmer of a smile softened his face.

"Thanks again for the directions you gave me this morning, Miss Hubbard. They led me straight to that meal I was needing so badly, and also to a job. Gib Dawson sends his best and hopes you'll come visiting him again like you used to, riding a little paint pony."

Color whipped across Stewart Hubbard's face, but she did not answer. Stagmire tipped his head again to her, but before he could leave there came the sound of brisk, solid steps in the outer office and then a big man with heavy shoulders, a florid face, and a shock of tawny hair came in.

For a moment pure surprise held Ruel Tedrow. He stared at Stagmire, then switched his glance to Jared Hubbard questioningly. Hubbard spoke with open satisfaction.

"Glad you happened in, Ruel. For this fellow here has been giving me some intolerable nonsense to the effect that we are feeding stolen beef to our logging and mill crews. Of course I don't believe him and I've told him so. Have you anything to add?"

"Yes, Mister Hubbard, I have," rapped Tedrow. "And I'll deliver it in my own way if you don't mind." He whirled on Stagmire, anger brushing across the broad ruddiness of his face, his shoulders swinging with hard, truculent arrogance.

"Listen, you! There's been a lot of that loose talk about stolen beef going around, and I'm heartily sick and tired of it. I buy every pound of beef that goes on the tables of our crews and I happen to know it's honest beef. Now I don't know what penny-ante, two-bit rancher you're putting up your howl for, but I do know that you're peddling lies. And if I hear any more of them, then somebody is going to be hurt . . . bad!"

Wade Stagmire looked Ruel Tedrow up and

down with a flat, cold stare. He spoke almost softly. "Mister, I hear a big wind blowing. Go easy with calling someone a liar. We'll let it pass this time because we're where we are and with other people present. But go easy. *¿Comprende?*"

Ruel Tedrow had come up in the Hubbard organization the hard way and had left his mark on many a rough-and-tumble logger or mill hand. There was nothing in the physical way about this lean, brown cowboy to give him much pause, but there was a certain something in that cowboy's eyes that told Tedrow to leave well enough alone. For one of the few real whippings Tedrow had ever receipted for in his life came at the hands of a man who had that same wickedly cold glint in his eyes, and Tedrow had never forgotten it. Sheer spirit could make a lot of things even, it seemed.

It was Jared Hubbard who gave Ruel Tedrow a chance to back away gracefully.

"We'll leave any talk of violence out of this, Ruel. The charge is, of course, preposterous, and I can fully understand why you should be angry about it. Such talk is annoying, but as long as there is nothing to it, we can afford to ignore it. I hope, Mister Stagmire, that you are now fully satisfied that there is nothing to your outrageous claim. You have my word for it and you have Mister Tedrow's to back mine up." Then Hubbard added, dryly sarcastic: "As I said twice before, our business is lumbering, not cattle rustling. Good day, Mister Stagmire."

Wade Stagmire measured Jared Hubbard again with a long, quiet glance, then nodded slightly as though confirming some judgment of his own. "Thanks for listening to me, Mister Hubbard," he said, as he turned and went out.

Ruel Tedrow stared at the closed door for a moment, then turned to Hubbard. "That fellow showed up in the slash above the Sotoyome River this morning. He was grublining then, asking directions. Now he's in here talking like he had something to say. I don't get it."

"Apparently," said Jared Hubbard, "he's taken on with Gib Dawson and was speaking for him. And I don't like what he had to say. Ruel, are you certain that Frank Lawrey's cattle operations are strictly legitimate?"

Tedrow gave a short, scoffing laugh. "Of course, Mister Hubbard. Here's the picture. Frank Lawrey has a fat contract, supplying us with beef. Every cattleman in this part of the country is envious of him, wishing they had such a contract. And, human nature being what it is, they never lose a chance to throw rocks at him. Their talk doesn't mean a thing."

Jared Hubbard looked down at his desk thoughtfully, drummed fingertips upon it. "I still don't like it," he observed. "The reputation of our organization means too much to me to have it impugned in any way, even indirectly. Perhaps we'd be wise to spread our beef buying around a little more. That should stop any careless talk."

Ruel Tedrow shook his head. "I doubt it. Any organization as big as the Hubbard Lumbering Company is going to be talked about by little men, regardless. As for the beef supply angle, I don't think we'd be at all wise to change it. As things stand now we have a reliable, steady source of supply. Lawrey has built up things in such a manner as to guarantee unfailing delivery of whatever amount we need, exactly when we need it. That's important in keeping our loggers and mill hands well fed and happy. If we tried to bring some little, one-horse cow outfits into the picture, maybe we'd get our beef when we needed it and . . . maybe we wouldn't. They might start haggling for higher prices, or something. Then we'd have nothing but trouble. I think you must agree that it is much more efficient this way."

Jared Hubbard nodded slowly. "No doubt of it. And I suppose being the object of a certain amount of careless gossip is one of the unavoidable penalties of being big. However," he added, with just a hint of a wry smile, "being accused of cattle rustling, even indirectly, was a brand-new experience."

Chapter Six

Gib Dawson hunched over the supper table, cradling his coffee cup in both gnarled hands and peering at Wade Stagmire from under frosty, shaggy brows.

"You mean you actually tackled Jared Hubbard in his own private office. Son, how'd you manage it?"

Stagmire shrugged. "Just followed my nose until I found him. As long as I was in Castle City, I figured it was worth the try to get at our trouble through him. But I didn't have much luck. He was plenty emphatic about only honest beef being served to his crews."

"Hah," grunted Gib Dawson. "We know better. Sometimes I wonder if he's as honest as I think he is. What's your guess?"

Stagmire considered a moment, soberly thoughtful. "That's a pretty big layout he's the head of, Gib. No man could have his finger on all the details of a business that size. He has to trust somebody to take care of some things for him . . . and he trusts Ruel Tedrow."

"Would you?"

Stagmire smiled grimly, shook his head. "I don't like Mister Ruel Tedrow . . . don't like him at all. Nobody has a right to any opinion but

Mister Tedrow. He's out to make you take his word for a thing even if he has to beat your head in."

"Ruel Tedrow is crooked," declared Gib Dawson flatly. "But make no mistake about it . . . he's a rough, tough customer. He didn't climb to where he is by being any gentle lily. A damn' mean man in a fight, that feller."

"Stewart Hubbard was there," said Stagmire, smiling a little. "I told her you sent your best and hoped she'd come riding out to visit you again."

"What did she say to that?"

"She didn't say a word. That was just before Tedrow came in. I may be wrong in this, but somehow I had the feeling when I first went into Hubbard's office that he and his niece had been having a little argument about something and that Hubbard had come out second best."

Gib Dawson chuckled. "He'd probably been trying to make up Stewart's mind for her about something. You'd think he'd've learned better by this time. For nobody makes up that girl's mind on anything except herself. She always was an independent little monkey. Her and me, we sure used to get along fine."

Stagmire, finished with his supper, leaned back and rolled a smoke. "Saw Bill Vessels in town."

Gib Dawson straightened in his chair. "The hell. How'd that happen?"

Stagmire sketched briefly the affair in the

Cattleman saloon. Dawson swore softly. "So you sided Bill Vessels against Price Mabry and those two whelps, Gentry and Krug, eh? Boy, that Mabry's a bad one."

"So Vessels said," Stagmire agreed. "Gib, we may have Vessels and Harley Jacks and Buck Hare back with us."

Dawson's deep eyes gleamed. "You really think there's a chance?"

"Yeah, I do. Their cattle ranch deal in Wind Pike Valley has gone bust, according to Vessels. They've been rustled blind. And Vessels is certain Frank Lawrey is responsible. I think I sold Vessels on the idea of tying in with Anchor again, so we could fight Lawrey together."

"Son, I hope so!" exclaimed Dawson. "I'm plumb ready to eat plenty of humble crow if those boys will only drop their saddles here again."

That night Wade Stagmire slept in a real bed again for the first time in weeks. It had been a long and eventful day. The start had hardly been auspicious; it had been a cold, hungry and friendless one. And then Stagmire had happened to ride into the slash where the big redwood was being felled, and there had met a girl with raven-black hair and lovely gray eyes, and she had given him trail directions that led to a swift and agreeable change in the state of his affairs.

It seemed, he mused sleepily, that his luck had changed the moment he first met Stewart

Hubbard. This was a pleasant thought and he was considering it when Noyo, the Indian, came quietly into the bunkhouse and closed the door against a damp, chill wind that had begun to blow, throwing its moist breath blustering about the buildings of the ranch.

"Fog tomorrow morning," said Noyo, as he went along to his bunk.

Noyo knew his weather. Wade Stagmire dressed the next morning in a chill, gray half light, then stepped out of the bunkhouse into a world muffled and drowned in dripping mists. It was as though a great, wet, wool fleece had been lowered against the earth, through which Stagmire had almost to feel his way to the cook shack where Noyo, already up and busy, had breakfast going. Gib Dawson came in, his crutch creaking.

"Rustler's delight, this cussed fog," growled the old fellow. "Them who know the country and the trails could run off with half a ranch and you'd never know it was gone until the sun came out again."

Noyo poured a cup of steaming coffee, held it out to Dawson, who, after the first long swallow, began to thaw. "Fog's good for the grass, though," he amended, his tone milder. "Keeps it green along the slopes."

Noyo glanced at Stagmire, a faint smile touching his brown, impassive face. Stagmire grinned back. Noyo knew how to open the day for his boss.

As they sat down to eat, Gib Dawson asked: "You got any special ideas for the day, son?"

"Thought I'd do a little ranching," Stagmire said. "Get acquainted with the country and the lay of Anchor range. Also get a line on our cattle."

"Good idea," agreed Dawson. "We take in all this valley and over the next ridge north as far as Hester Creek. The valley range is the best, of course, but that to the north ain't so bad, either. You get across the ridge and you run into heavy timber . . . a stand of redwoods so big they'll knock your eye out. But on the south slope of the ridge there's plenty of open country. And the cattle seem to like it there. Mebbe because it's warmer. That ridge on the south of the valley, the one you came in over yesterday morning, that's all Hubbard timber holdings and they've been cutting heavy up there."

Dawson paused, taking a big drag at his coffee cup.

"The stand of redwood that falls inside our line over along Hester Creek, there's plenty of board feet in it . . . plenty! I reckon Hubbard would like to own that stand. Fact is, one day a while back, Ruel Tedrow stopped in here and wanted to know what I'd take for it. The damn' gall of him, with him working in cahoots with a guy that's out to rustle me off the face of the earth.

I sure told that jigger where to go, y'betcha."

"In the past, just how has Frank Lawrey's crowd worked against you, Gib?" Stagmire asked. "I mean before Trautwine and Krug and Gentry took to selling you out?"

Dawson shrugged. "Just about any way he could pick up a jag of cows and get clear with them. On their own the cattle don't get into the timber much. Not enough feed there. But they graze all along the edge of it. Not much of a trick for some of Lawrey's crowd to prowl just inside the timber, spot some cattle feeding close in, make a quick gather of fifteen or twenty head, put 'em back along some timber trail, and haze 'em on out to the coast."

"Those cattle would leave a trail, that's certain," said Stagmire.

"Uhn-huh," grunted the cattleman, "they sure would. But the trouble is, time you miss 'em and pick up that trail, they're long gone."

"Yet you could still follow it and it would have to lead somewhere," argued Stagmire.

"Sure it would. It'd lead right out to some cove or headland, and there it'd end. No cattle . . . no nothing. Oh, I know what you're thinking, son . . . which is that the cattle, wherever they were, would still be packing an Anchor brand. But it ain't that simple. Now when I first began losing cows and figgered it out that Lawrey was the man responsible, I made me a trip, bum leg and all, down to his Wagon Wheel outfit. I demanded the right to look around. Lawrey, damn his slippery soul, was polite and agreeable as all hell. He even hooked up a buckboard and drove me all over his ranch himself. He knew what I was looking for and he knew I wouldn't find any. Anchor brands, I mean. Because that wasn't the way he was working on me."

Dawson paused to eat a little of his food. He waved a fork. "I came up with the answer, later. Take a day like this one, with this fog. Back here, inland, chances are the fog will thin out by noon and the sun begin to shine. But out on the coast proper it'll be thick as soup and may lay that way for days at a time. All right. Lawrey sees that a fog is due. He sends out some of his fine thieves to get at their dirty work. They lift a jag of Anchor cows and chouse 'em out to the coast. They make an open slaughter of them, on some beach or rocky headland. They got the cover of the fog to work in. They skin out the carcasses, chuck the hides and offal into the sea. If they've worked on a beach, the tide comes in and wipes out all sign. If they've operated on a headland, well there might be a little blood sign, but it don't last long, not with the fog drenching things and the spume flying in the fog wind.

"So then Lawrey has a wagon handy, mebbe two or three wagons. The meat is hauled in to the cold house he's got in Castle City, where it's hung up for a time before it's distributed to Hubbard's camps and boarding houses. With the hide off, beef's beef. We can't prove a damn' thing. You can't walk into Lawrey's cold room, point to a side of beef, and say it's Anchor beef. You got no hide to shake out. You got nothing. So there you have it, son. That beef ain't cost Lawrey a damn' cent outside the small expense of running it off, slaughtering it, and hanging it. Nice profit for him in that kind of business."

Stagmire, finished eating, twisted up a cigarette, his eyes narrowed with thought. "You paint a tough deal to stop, for a fact," he admitted. "Proving ownership under those conditions would be mean, even if Jared Hubbard was open to be convinced, which right now he doesn't seem to be. We're going to have to get right down to fundamentals, Gib. We've got to do our best to catch the thieves in the act and then really work them over."

The old cattleman nodded emphatically. "That's right. Catch 'em cold and put the fear of God into them. But that won't be easy to do, son. I tell you, Frank Lawrey's a fox."

Stagmire went out to catch and saddle. It was still a gray, wet world, but the fog had begun to thin a little here around headquarters. Even so, when Stagmire dropped down to the river and headed east along it, working inland through the valley, a scant hundred yards was about the limit of vision.

The fog seemed to restrict sound as well as sight. Stagmire rode through a muffled world, hearing only the subdued thump of his horse's hoofs and the vaguest of faint splashing where the river foamed over a shallows. Birds, startled by Stagmire's ghostly approach, flitted away, voiceless. Little bunches of cattle, stirring from bedding grounds, were real one moment, then vanishing phantoms the next.

Stagmire kept to the flats until the valley began pinching in, the black mass of timber looming on his right and sharply pitched downward, but open slopes on his left. He reined left and angled up these slopes. He struck a narrow cattle trail that wound and twisted, crossing low points and ridges, slicing through sweeping gulches, but always gradually climbing.

He took his time, letting his horse set its own gait. There was no rush in what he was about. A man, committed to what could very well become a battleground in the immediate future, was smart to learn the lay of the land. It was important that he get the feel of the country, for it was this that could give him a sense of proper direction, even if he rode it in the black of night or through a gray fog blanket such as this one.

Here on this open slope, Stagmire began meeting up with more and more cattle. They grazed on long-running benches, in sweeping, sheltered hollows, and once, head on, he met a file of them going down to the river to drink. They scattered, letting him through, drifting past him on both sides, and the fog swallowed them up behind him. The bawl of a critter echoed shortly along the slope, a muffled, lonely sound.

In time, as he continued this upward, circling climb, Stagmire moved out of a world of hovering stillness. Here the fog was no longer a motionless thing, but began streaming past in long, wet banners. For up here there was a wind blowing, sliding in from the sea, whipping the fog ahead of it. That wind brought a chill and Stagmire, now heading west along the north rim of the valley, began dropping lower and lower as he rode, until finally the wind was well above him and he was down in a still, gray world once more.

He knew he had circled well above Anchor headquarters and that the ranch buildings now lay some three or four miles behind him to the east. Soon the valley would begin pinching in again to timbered ridges, between which the Sotoyome River flowed to the sea. Now, of a sudden, Stagmire picked up sounds. The first, from far up on the south ridge where Hubbard's loggers were working, came as a booming, rumbling crash. And Stagmire knew that another towering giant of the redwood forest had gone down before the keen bite of axe and saw.

Yet it was a different sound, which came shortly after, that really focused Stagmire's attention. The bawl of a cow critter. Not the casual plaint of an animal momentarily lost or separated from its fellows in the fog, but the sharper, more harried protest of an animal being driven faster than its usual habit of travel. Stagmire reared in his saddle, fixed the direction of the sound as nearly as he could, which was below and ahead of him. He heard it a second time and lifted his horse to a run.

He was closer to the river than he thought. Within two hundred yards he hit the town trail and raced along it. A moment later he had his horse set back almost on its haunches, for a mounted figure loomed in the fog, holding the middle of the trail. Stagmire instinctively started for his gun, but stopped the move halfway, feeling a little foolish. The rider was Stewart Hubbard.

She was up on a clean-limbed sorrel and she sat her saddle erectly and well. She was in a divided skirt of dark twill and her scarlet Mackinaw was buttoned to the throat. She was bare of head and her raven hair was beaded with a fine silver mist of fog moisture. Her gray eyes were wide and startled at Stagmire's sudden, headlong approach. Yet she was alert and thinking, for she twisted in her saddle and pointed.

"I heard it, too!" she exclaimed. "Over there!

79

Somebody is harrying cattle. No riders with you?"

"No," rapped Stagmire, recovering from his surprise, and knowing a quick surge of satisfaction because of her swift recognition of him. "Not with me. This could be what I was talking to your uncle about, yesterday afternoon. Now I've got to see!"

He raced past her, digging in the spurs, following where she had pointed. Within a hundred yards he was up against a wall of timber, reared black and dripping in front of him. He pulled up again, standing high and twisted in his stirrups, listening. In the dank timber ahead of him he heard it again, muffled now. An animal's bawl of protest. He sent his horse plunging into the dim fastnesses of the redwoods.

It was dripping and ghostly in here, for the fog had sifted down and the towering trees lifted up and lost their lofty crests in it. Dodging massive trunks, Stagmire sent his mount slashing through thickets of giant fern that sprayed fog moisture and swiftly drenched him to the skin.

He saw movement ahead. Cattle! A rider—two riders. This time he went for his gun in earnest. He yelled, his voice puny in the smother of fog and brooding timber. Yet it carried far enough. One of those riders came around. A gun boomed, its report pressed down to an echoless thud. A sliver of bark spun off the trunk of a tree beside Stagmire. So now he was sure.

The gun that had been Gib Dawson's belted its challenge twice, the recoil heavy and solid and satisfying in Stagmire's fist. Gun flame, thinly pale in the murk and gloom, whipped back at him. Stagmire shot again, and the figure behind that gun flame fell forward along the neck of his horse, balanced there for a moment, then slithered limply off. The second rider raced off to one side, shouting a hard summons.

Stagmire went after him, lost him in the tangle. Cattle, eight or ten of them, held closely bunched up to now, scattered like a covey of startled quail. Gunfire broke from three different points ahead of Stagmire, and he held back a little against such odds, wary of running into an ambush. Yet a wave of cold exultation whipped through him. This was obviously another raid on Anchor cattle and he had broken it up.

Under him he could feel the rapid lift and fall of his horse's hard breathing, and, while his eyes probed and searched the fog gloom in the timber, he reloaded the empty chambers of his gun. He sent his mount ahead at a walk, alert for anything that moved. He glimpsed the indistinct outline of rider and mount and shot swiftly, and knew he had missed.

Guns hammered to both his right and left and his horse reared, shaking. As it came down, he sensed a queer breaking up of the animal's strength and co-ordination and he knew it had been mortally hit. He kicked free of the stirrups and threw himself clear as the horse went down. He sprawled on the wet cushion of the forest mold and the stark realization hit him that the small exultation he'd known just a moment before had been entirely premature.

He rolled away from the dying but still struggling horse, came up against a tree, got to his knees, then fully to his feet behind the tree's protection. But the raiders had him located and the flat and heavy thudding of guns beat ominously through the timber and lead whipped sullenly into the tree.

He knew that this tree would offer only a temporary respite from the raiders' fire. They'd soon be working around on each side of him and get him in a crossfire. He wondered bleakly if his luck could have run out on him so quickly and finally?

He crouched close against the tree, waiting, head swinging as he tried to watch both sides. He was looking to the right when the shot sounded to his left. He felt the bullet tug at his clothes across the small of his back. That close had the slug come.

He drove an answering shot, throwing it blindly, for he saw no target. Then he dived back beside his horse, now dead and completely still. For the bulk of the animal would at least protect him fully on one flank while he watched ahead and to the other. And being close to the earth this way offered him another advantage. He would be a less distinct target to the raiders than they to him, for they would be up in the saddle.

Gunfire ceased for a moment and deeply aching silence held. Earth's damp breath came up to Stagmire, strong with the mold of centuries. He waited, eyes and ears straining. Abruptly a gun coughed and a bullet thudded into the bulk of the horse. Stagmire made no move to fire back. He waited, motionless, breath taut in his throat. Two more bullets chunked into the horse, one from each side and the one that had come from the right, had it been a foot lower, would have torn into Stagmire's shoulder. The net was tightening.

On his left, Stagmire was blind, for there the mounted stillness of the horse lay. For all he knew, one or several of the raiders could be crawling up on him from that side, but he could not take the chance of rising up for a look, for that would expose him fully to the raider on his right. He had to wait this thing out, hope for some sort of break.

Again the gun to his right boomed and a clot of forest mold humped and spattered just a yard beyond Stagmire and in front of him. Somehow, the way the stuff flew, it gave him a line to look along, which was a little to the rear as well as to the right. And he saw his man, afoot, darting from the protection of one tree to another. Stagmire lifted his gun, waited.

He saw the fellow edge into view, not thirty yards away. And, shadowy and indistinct as things were in this fog-shrouded timber, Stagmire recognized this man. It was Rocky Gentry!

Until this moment, Stagmire had known no particular anger in this affair. He recognized it as a grim duel, another bald rustling stroke against Gib Dawson, which he'd been lucky to break up, but which had left him in as tight a spot as he'd ever known. He had swapped lead with the raiders and seen one man go down before his gun. But up until now there had been something almost impersonal about it all, a fight against men so shadowy in the wet murk as to be almost unreal.

Now it was different. Yonder was Rocky Gentry, once an Anchor hand himself, a traitorous one, and proving at this moment that he'd gone fully over to the enemy. This injected a new note into the business and stirred a cold and wicked anger in Stagmire. He pushed up on his left elbow to get a clearer view of Gentry.

The move caught Gentry's eye and he threw a blindingly fast shot. Stagmire felt the lead burn across his ribs and the shock drove him back against the bulk of the dead animal he lay beside. He rocked up again on his left elbow, gun pushed level and questing. He saw Rocky Gentry across the sights of the weapon, saw Gentry chopping down for another try.

Stagmire had a strange sense of deliberateness about his own shot—of taking tremendous care with it. The muzzle of his gun steadied, then leaped up as the weapon bucked in recoil, momentarily blotting out his target. Then it dropped down once more and Stagmire could see Gentry again.

Rocky Gentry was down on his knees, bent forward. His hands were pawing aimlessly at the forest mold in front of him, as though he were looking for something he'd lost. Then he salaamed very low, fell over on the point of his right shoulder, flattened out, and was still.

A bitter and rage-thinned yell cut through the timber, carrying on it the first distinct words Stagmire had heard since this affair began.

"Rush him . . . everybody! Rush that damned proud . . . !" The words ran out in a burst of scalding profanity.

Stagmire drew his knees up under him, ready to lunge one way or the other. This was to be it.

Chapter Seven

Wade Stagmire waited for the rush to materialize, waited and watched. At no time had he been sure of the exact number of the raiders and he had no idea what the odds would be now. He could see the stir, the gather of movement in the timber. Men who had left their horses, the better to stalk their quarry, now went back into their saddles, to utilize the speed of their horses in an overwhelming charge. Stagmire could glimpse this shadowed movement, guessed its purpose, but held his fire, not wanting to waste lead at this distance.

He waited—while the warm slime of blood ran down his creased ribs and he was suddenly thirsty and a faint tremor of weakness ran through him, putting a quake in the muscles of his legs and leaving his midriff feeling all hollow and gaunt. The harshness of utter desperation pulled across his face and his fist tightened about the butt of his gun. He'd sell out dearly in this thing, right down to the last cartridge, the last drive of strength and vitality. . . .

Increasing movement flickered in the dripping aisles of the timber, both ahead and behind him. Now came that thin and wild yell again, but this time carrying a note of surprise and warning. The rush from in front failed utterly to show and all movement that way was suddenly gone.

Stagmire twisted to face the rear. Three riders there, coming up fast. He threw up his gun, but held fire, for the shout that came out ahead of these three carried his name.

"Stagmire! Show yourself, man! Oh, Stagmire!"

He hauled to his feet, hardly understanding. They saw him and came plunging up. Stagmire dropped his gun hand to his side, put the other against a tree for support.

"Vessels," he mumbled stupidly. "Bill Vessels . . ."

It was Bill Vessels, right enough, raw-boned, reckless of eye. He swooped from his saddle, eyes bleak with concern. "You're hit, man! How bad . . . ?"

Stagmire grinned crookedly. "Still on my feet, but a mite shaky. Mister, you look good to me. It was beginning to get grim. Whatever brought you here?"

"Taking you at your word that Gib Dawson wanted us back. We were coming in along the river trail and ran across that Hubbard girl. She told us you'd gone in here alone . . . and why. Then we heard shooting and figgered you might need a hand. Meet Harley Jacks and Buck Hare. Boys, this is Wade Stagmire, that I was telling you about."

Harley Jacks was a redhead, lanky, freckled,

with big ears and a grin to match. Buck Hare was of medium height, compactly built, slightly swarthy, with a quiet, level-eyed competency about him. His voice was soft, even, unhurried.

"You get a good look at any of them, Stagmire?"

"One," answered Stagmire. "Rocky Gentry. He's down . . . yonder. Then there's another one, back nearer the edge of the timber somewhere. He was the first I ran into."

"Now then, that's interesting!" exclaimed Harley Jacks. "Let's have a look, Buck."

They spun their horses away, threading the timber. Bill Vessels stayed with Stagmire, saying: "Sit down. Let's have a look at you."

He helped Stagmire out of his jumper and shirt, had a look at the wound. "You've lost some blood," he growled, "and you'll be sore as a boil for a few days. This will last until we get to Anchor headquarters where we can do a real job on it."

By the time Stagmire was back into his shirt and jumper, Harley Jacks and Buck Hare rode up, leading a couple of saddle mounts. "Gentry's and Vidal's," said Buck Hare.

"Mogy Vidal, eh?" declared Bill Vessels. "Be damned! Now that's good riddance. And also proof positive of who tried the raid. Stagmire will need one of those horses. I'll take him back to headquarters, and then come back and meet you boys here. I'll bring digging tools."

Stagmire grimaced as he swung up onto

the horse that had been Rocky Gentry's. That wounded side was really beginning to hurt. He nodded toward the horse that lay dead, just beyond. "That saddle . . . it's a good one. I've had it a long time."

"Sure," said Buck Hare. "We'll bring it up to the ranch for you."

The world was much lighter when they broke from the timber and regained the river trail. The fog had begun to thin and lift. And Stewart Hubbard was there, waiting on the trail. Stagmire, riding hunched over to ease the pain in his wounded side, straightened as her swift glance touched him, but this did not fool her at all. Her voice was low, a little breathless.

"You've been hurt . . . ?"

Stagmire's smile was lopsided. "Scratch across the ribs . . . not much. A lot of thanks for directing Vessels and the other two boys in there, Miss Hubbard."

"That's not the horse you rode . . . going in," she said.

"Circumstances made me swap," he explained, trying to keep his tone light.

But he saw that he wasn't keeping any grim information from this girl. She was entirely too observing and shrewd for that. She got the picture, all right. She knew that somebody had died, back in that dark, dank timber. She bit at a red underlip, looking away.

"It was . . . rustling?" she asked.

Bill Vessels took over, a little blunt. "That's right. Some of Frank Lawrey's crowd, trying another raid on Anchor cattle. But this one they didn't get away with. Stagmire broke it up. Now let's get along to headquarters."

The girl seemed to hesitate a little, undecided whether to go along with them, or turn back. Stagmire made up her mind for her. "Old Gib . . . he sure will be tickled to see you again, Miss Hubbard."

So, as he and Bill Vessels moved off, Stewart Hubbard fell in behind and followed.

The horses were throwing faint shadows by the time they reached headquarters—the sun was that close to breaking completely through the thinning overcast. Stewart Hubbard turned off at the ranch house, but Bill Vessels kept on to the bunkhouse, where he gave Stagmire a hand in dismounting and getting him inside to a bunk. Stagmire lay back with a long sigh, his face carved and drawn, his eyes closed.

"Hell of a note," he grumbled. "A grown man feeling limp as a kitten just because of a scratch across the ribs."

Bill Vessels snorted profanely. "What do you figger is necessary to put a man on his back . . . loss of both arms and a leg? Now you take it plumb easy while I scare up some hot water."

In the end it was the Indian, Noyo, who did the

real doctoring job on Stagmire. Noyo washed away the blood, cleaned the wound thoroughly, then daubed it with some black, pungent mixture all his own, and bandaged it firmly with strips of clean cloth. With Vessels helping, Noyo got Stagmire between blankets, gave him a drink of water and a cupful of some kind of bitter brew he'd concocted.

"You sleep now," said the Indian quietly.

"Not now, Noyo," argued Stagmire. "Got a lot of things to talk over."

"You sleep," said Noyo again, and with a serene certainty.

Noyo knew what he was talking about, knew the potency of that bitter mixture. Stagmire grew swiftly drowsy and presently was deep in sleep, the lines in his face softening and smoothing out.

Noyo looked at Vessels. "You come back to stay?"

Vessels nodded. "That's right, Noyo. Buck and Harley, too."

"Good!" said the Indian. "Now this a real outfit again." He looked at Stagmire. "A good man. Damn' good man!"

"No argument there," growled Vessels. "He sure put a crimp in Lawrey's crowd this day."

Vessels left the bunkhouse, began gathering up a pick and a couple of shovels. Gib Dawson stumped out to the ranch house porch and called to him. Vessels went over.

"How is he?" asked Dawson.

"Sleeping. Give him a few days and he'll be as good as new. You got yourself a real hand there, Gib."

The old cattleman nodded. "I know that. I figger to have more. Bill, I've been a damned old fool where you and Harley and Buck are concerned. I don't deserve it, but if you boys will come back with me, you got jobs as long as this ranch holds together. Cuss me out if it'll make you feel better, then we'll hit hands on a new shake all around."

"Misunderstandings crop up in the best of outfits," said Vessels gruffly. "The one we had is all cleared up now. Me and Harley and Buck . . . we're glad to be back. Miss Hubbard tell you about this morning's fracas?"

"Some," admitted Dawson. "Only what she knew, which wasn't all, I guess."

"Stagmire got two of them," Vessels said. "Rocky Gentry and Mogy Vidal. Now there's a fine pair of snakes that won't be slithering around underfoot no more. Yeah, Stagmire got both of 'em and busted up the raid to boot. That'll give Lawrey and Ruel Tedrow something to think about."

Gib Dawson lifted a warning finger to his lips, threw a swift glance over his shoulder. "Now you're right there, of course, Bill," he rumbled softly. "But we must be careful of Stewart's ears.

She's the same fine youngster as always."

Pick and shovels balanced across his saddle, Bill Vessels rode away downriver to where Harley Jacks and Buck Hare waited for him. Gib Dawson went back into the ranch house. Stewart Hubbard stood at a window, watching Bill Vessels's disappearing figure. Abruptly she turned to Dawson.

"Now we will get at a few facts, Mister Gib." She had called him that when she was just a long-legged youngster, years before, and it was something that had always tickled the grim old ranchman. Now the same address fell from her lips with complete naturalness. "The first fact is that I'm no longer a child, to be fed fairy stories. So remember that, when you answer the questions I'm going to ask you. That affair this morning . . . men were killed?"

"Two of them," Dawson told her gravely. "Trying to rustle my cows, they were. Wade Stagmire, my new rider, took care of that. It was one of those things. The boy had no other out. It was them or him, I reckon. He's a plenty good hand, Wade Stagmire is."

"The rustlers . . . do you think they were working for Frank Lawrey?"

"No question, youngster. Rocky Gentry was one of three riders who were selling me out to Lawrey through Price Mabry. And Mogy Vidal, he's been a Wagon Wheel hand ever since he hit this country. Yeah, it's a mortal cinch that Lawrey was behind the raid."

"Gentry and Vidal," said the girl slowly and gravely. "They were the two who were killed?"

"That's right," said Dawson, showing some discomfort. "But this ain't no way pleasant talk for you, youngster. It's over and done with now. So let's you and me talk of better things. Me, I been wanting to hear about all the things you did when you were away at school. I bet you had plenty good times. You sure grew up pretty, lassie. And you got no idea how lonesome I used to get for you."

Her fine eyes softened a little as she looked at him. This grim, fierce old fellow had never been anything but kind and gentle with her and had always seemed to show her a deeper understanding than had her uncle, Jared Hubbard.

"I missed you, too, Mister Gib," she told him. "Oh, the schooling was all right and I guess I needed it badly. But that wasn't my country and the people, though they were very nice to me, simply weren't my kind of people. They spoke a different language in a different world. More than once I got so homesick I crawled off in a corner to weep. But now, we still have some questions to ask and be answered."

She paused, frowning a little. Then she squared her shoulders, as though ready to accept the worst. "Yesterday afternoon, your new rider,

Wade Stagmire, stood in Uncle Jared's office and said flatly that Hubbard loggers and mill hands were being fed stolen beef . . . some of it Anchor beef. What is your opinion?"

Gib Dawson stumped over to the table, got his pipe, loaded and lit it. He felt the girl's glance following him and he knew there wasn't any way out of this thing. He couldn't hedge or dodge the issue. This fine girl, even though the truth hurt, deserved the truth. He looked at her through a rolling cloud of tobacco smoke and spoke with sober gruffness.

"The boy was carrying my own thoughts and beliefs to your uncle, Stewart."

"You have proof of any sort, Mister Gib?"

"No," admitted the old fellow. "None of the kind that would stand up in court, mebbe. For after a hide carrying a man's brand is off a butchered beef . . . off and destroyed . . . all legal proof is gone. Who's to identify a haunch of hung beef? But I do know that Frank Lawrey's crowd have been rustling Anchor cattle and I know that Frank Lawrey supplies the beef that feeds Hubbard loggers and mill hands. So there's got to be some kind of connection there."

Stewart Hubbard turned and stared out of the window again. "If Hubbard employees are eating stolen beef, Mister Gib . . . do you believe Uncle Jared knows about it?"

"No," answered Gib Dawson with quick

emphasis and sincerity. "Once I wondered, but not any more. And Wade Stagmire, after talking with your uncle, said he was just about certain that Jared Hubbard has no idea of such a thing. After all, your uncle has bigger things on his mind than running a commissary. He leaves that up to them working for him."

"In which case, that would be Ruel Tedrow," the girl said. "Do you believe that Ruel Tedrow knows he's buying stolen beef from Frank Lawrey?" She came around to face him, her gray eyes intent.

Gib Dawson nodded decisively. "Youngster, I got to say I do. I'll go further. I'll bet my life that he does. I'm sorry it's that way, but . . ."

"Don't be sorry, Mister Gib," she cut in quickly. "I asked for an answer . . . and the truth. Thank you for telling me. Now . . . we'll talk of the old days."

Chapter Eight

Wade Stagmire slept all the rest of the day and through the following night. He awakened in the gray dawn of another foggy morning. His wounded side was stiff and sore, but otherwise he felt amazingly renewed. And hungry as a wolf.

Looking around, he saw that he was alone in the bunkhouse and he was thinking about getting up and into his clothes when Noyo came in. The Indian, reading Stagmire's thought, shook a reproving head.

"You stay there two more days. Then you get up."

"Where's Bill Vessels and the others?" asked Stagmire.

"Out early, riding," informed Noyo. "Fog time... thief time. No good! You hungry?"

"Plenty."

Noyo showed his rare grin. "Good! You eat here. I bring it."

Propped up in his bunk, Stagmire had just finished eating a solid breakfast when Gib Dawson came in, his crutch stumping. He sat down on an adjoining bunk and showed Stagmire a grim smile.

"This looks good to me, son . . . . you sitting up cocky as a jaybird and taking on nourishment.

You put a kink in them, didn't you? That's just about the first time that one of Lawrey's raids ever backfired. That's going to slow that crowd down."

"Maybe," said Stagmire briefly. "But just slowing them down ain't enough, Gib."

The cattleman cocked a grizzled head. "There's two meanings to that. You got something on your mind."

Stagmire built a cigarette. "It was luck, their bad, our good . . . not smart thinking on our part that busted up that raid, Gib. If I'd happened to be fifteen minutes later getting to where I happened to be, I'd never have heard that critter bawl and so gone to investigate. If they'd shot a little straighter, I'd have been dead. If Bill Vessels and Jacks and Hare hadn't happened along and Miss Hubbard been there to tell them where I was, and why, then I'd have been dead anyhow. Lot of ifs all through it, Gib. And you can't run a ranch on ifs."

"No, you can't," admitted Dawson slowly, getting out his pipe. "Have your say. I'm listening."

Stagmire was soberly thoughtful for a moment, letting blue smoke curl from his lips. Then he stirred restlessly.

"I'm still too new here to get all the picture. But from what you've told me I gather you've been fighting what might be called a defensive

100

war against Frank Lawrey. And that ain't good. Fighting on defense means you're always one jump behind the other fellow, because he can pick his own time and place to hit you and you never know exactly when that time, or where that place, will be. Nobody ever won a war just sitting back and letting the enemy have first bite all the time. You keep on doing that and you end up with your head beat off. So, if this outfit is to keep on living and getting somewhere, we got to figure out a different answer, Gib."

Gib Dawson puffed furiously. Noyo, hovering at the bunkhouse door, bright-eyed and interested, nodded emphatic agreement to Stagmire's words.

"What is that different answer, son?" rumbled Dawson.

"That we carry the fight to Lawrey," Stagmire declared. "That we go after him, rough and tough and to a finish. That we bust him before he busts us."

Gib Dawson sat silently, eyes sober and thoughtful under their frosty, frowning brows. "A big chore," he said finally. "A damn' big chore, son. Lawrey's got five or six men where we got one. He's got a lot more money behind him than I have, and he's in strong with some parts of the Hubbard interests, which, when the chips are down, make the big power all along this stretch of coast. But, say I was willing to go along with your ideas, just how would you handle things?"

101

"How many cattle do you figure Lawrey's lifted off you, Gib?"

Dawson considered a moment, lips pursed. "If I said two hundred head, I wouldn't be too far wrong."

"That's a lot of cattle," rapped Stagmire. "Too many for you or anybody else to lose. And slow suicide if it keeps on. My idea is that we look Frank Lawrey in the eye, charge him openly with stealing those cows, and tell him we intend to get that many, or the value of that many back regardless. Make it cold turkey. Hit him hard. Jar him . . . shake him up. Let him know we're going to hold him personally responsible, that we don't intend to waste our strength just hitting at his hired hands, and that it's his scalp we lift if he doesn't replace the cattle he's stolen. And, then, that he leave us alone . . . complete!"

"He'd laugh at you, son," said Gib Dawson bluntly.

"And get the laugh knocked right back down his throat!" blazed Stagmire. There was no mistaking the fire of his feelings and Gib Dawson, seeing this, turned his tone almost gentle.

"You'd do just that, wouldn't you, son? And maybe you're right. Now, if I was twenty years younger and had two sound legs under me, I'd go along with you. But a man's got no right to ask others to do something for him that he ain't able to do for himself. Fight, I mean. Put their life on the line. I wouldn't want your blood on my conscience."

"You got some of it yesterday," reminded Stagmire. "And mighty close to all of it. How? By me riding patrol and trying to protect Anchor property. A man can be just as surely killed while trying to head off one of Lawrey's raids as he could by packing the fight right to Lawrey."

Gib Dawson stood up, tucked his crutch under his arm. His pipe was dead and his jaw set savagely on it. Abrupt anger burst from him.

"God damn it! All I ever asked of the world was to be left alone to run my ranch, with a few good men riding for me. Just so I made enough money to pay my crew good wages, feed 'em good, and have a happy outfit. Just this valley and my ranch and my boys. I never did yearn to be big as hell . . . and I don't want to now. All I ever asked was a small slice of life to be happy and contented in. And they won't let me have it. . . ."

The old cattleman broke off, looking a little sheepish. He stumped to the door and stood, looking out. When he spoke again, it was with a quiet gruffness. "I'll think on it, son. And I'll see what Bill Vessels and the other boys have to say about it."

Noyo stood at the bunkhouse door, watching

Gib Dawson plod his crutch-creaking way over to the ranch house.

"Him fine man," said the Indian softly. "Noyo go to hell for Gib Dawson."

Stagmire nodded soberly. "I know just what you mean, Noyo."

Chapter Nine

That night, grouped around Stagmire's bunk, the Anchor crew had a little council of war among themselves. Stagmire outlined his views, putting them up for the consideration of the others. Bill Vessels nodded immediate and vigorous assent.

"Only way to bring Lawrey to time is back him into a corner and kick his teeth in. We could go on patrolling this range until we grow moss on the back of our necks and we still couldn't keep Lawrey from lifting cows on us. Four men just can't be everywhere at once."

Harley Jacks, lanky and red-headed, grinned his agreement. Anything that suited Bill Vessels would always suit Harley. Buck Hare was in general agreement, but in his quiet, competent, brief-spoken way suggested some caution.

"It'll be a rough ride. We'll be way out-numbered. We'll be smart to figger all the angles. One thing is sure. Ruel Tedrow ain't thick with Frank Lawrey just because he loves him. And he ain't buying stolen beef from Lawrey just to make the books look good to Jared Hubbard. I'd bet plenty that Tedrow and Lawrey have a deal where Tedrow is getting an extra cut for his own pocket, somewhere."

"Say that's so," growled Vessels, "what's that got to do with us bracing Lawrey?"

"Like this," said Buck. "I don't know Jared Hubbard personal, but I've heard him discussed by plenty of others. And while I've heard it said that he's a tough one to handle in lots of ways, I've never heard any good man who really knew him claim that he wasn't square. So, before we go after Lawrey with the gloves off, I think we'd be smart to try and figure some way to prove to Jared Hubbard that Ruel Tedrow is crooked. Once we managed that, and Hubbard put the skids under Tedrow, that would leave Frank Lawrey way out on a lonesome limb where we could really get at him."

Every one of them knew there was nothing at all wrong with Buck Hare's nerve. They knew Buck wasn't cautioning this slower and more careful way because he was afraid of outright conflict. It was just that Buck was using his head.

Bill Vessels said: "Plenty of wisdom in that, Buck. But convincing Hubbard won't be easy. Ruel Tedrow is the fair-haired boy with Jared Hubbard."

Buck nodded. "I know that, Bill. But Jared Hubbard is a hard-headed businessman and mighty proud of the good name and reputation of his company. And those very things would make him mighty bitter against Tedrow, once he knows Tedrow's true color."

"I go along with Buck, there," said Stagmire. "He's heading down the right trail. That was what I had in mind when I braced Hubbard in his office the other day. I didn't get very far, I'll admit, but it could be that I planted the thought. Anyhow, it's one of the angles we'll have to work on. So now we'll wait and see what answer Gib Dawson arrives at when he gets his thinking done."

For the next two days things ran along quietly enough. Vessels, Hare, and Harley Jacks patrolled the range while Wade Stagmire grew increasingly restless from the confinement in his bunk. The morning of the third day, Noyo came in, took a look at the wounded side, grunted with satisfaction at the way it was healing, put a fresh bandage on it, and said briefly: "You get up now."

He helped Stagmire dress. Stagmire, moving with care, shaved, and then, holding himself stiffly erect, went over to the ranch house. It was a fine, bright morning, the spell of foggy weather gone, back here in this sheltered little valley. In the distance the timbered ridges drowsed in warm, blue mists and the clear slopes of the valley ran smoothly and cleanly and were dotted with grazing cattle. The picture of it all hit strongly home in Wade Stagmire. He'd been in this valley hardly a week, yet already he felt an affinity to it he'd never known for any chunk of range before. He thought of something Gib

Dawson had said: ". . . a small slice of life to be happy and contented in . . ."

Gib Dawson was sitting in the old rocker by his favorite window. He showed a small, grim smile. "Good to see you up and around again, son. The side pretty good?"

"Fine. Even beginning to itch. Noyo is one smart Indian. Well, Gib, you got your thinking done?"

The old cattleman turned grave. "Yeah, I have. Bill Vessels thinks your plan is right. So does Buck and Harley. Being as I'm outvoted, I guess I'll have to string along. And may the good Lord forgive me if I have to bury any of you boys. For I'll never forgive myself."

"Gib," said Stagmire gently, "you're trying to cross a whole flock of bridges that ain't anywhere in sight. It's a fine day. Soak it up and be happy in it."

Dawson, looking out the window, straightened. "You bet it's a fine day. For here comes my girl . . . riding. Now, ain't she a picture?"

He got no argument from Stagmire there. Stewart's black hair gleamed in the sun. Her scarlet Mackinaw was tied behind her saddle and the line of her throat, softly tanned, rising from the collar of her blouse, was faultless. Vivid reaction to the day's benevolence shone in her cheeks and lovely eyes. She swung from her sorrel mount with lithe ease and her step had a swing and exuberance in it as she crossed the porch and came in at the door, chattering with a little-girl eagerness.

"You wouldn't believe it, Mister Gib, but it's a bleak, raw day in town. But here, in your valley . . ."

She broke off, a little confused and coloring slightly at the sight of Stagmire. Looking at her, Stagmire thought that she had brought an immaculate shine into the room.

"Not my valley, lass," corrected Gib Dawson. "*Our* valley. And sort of empty and no-account until you come riding into it. My, oh, my, but we're pretty today. Makes me think of a patch of rhododendrons shining in the ferns. Come close to me, Stewart."

She moved over beside the old fellow's chair and he put a fond arm about her slenderness. "Now," he said, "my day's complete. I'm so rich it's shameful."

The girl flushed again, ran a slim hand through the old fellow's grizzled thatch. "Still spoiling me, like always. I can't stay long. Uncle Jared has some visitors up from San Francisco . . . big buyers, I think. I have to preside at dinner." Her glance touched Stagmire. "Your wound is better?"

"Thanks to Noyo," he answered.

The experience had thinned him a little, sharpened the square angles of his face, carving his features cleanly. But the strong beat of resurgent health showed under the deep weathered tan of his freshly shaven jaw. He looked finely tuned, competent.

Watching him, Stewart Hubbard pondered the make-up of men. He had left his gun in the bunkhouse, but she remembered him as he had looked with it on, spurring through the fog on the trail of the raiders. And two men had died before that big, black gun in the dripping timber. This lean, quiet cowboy had been behind that gun.

The thought of violent death was as repugnant to her as to any other normal member of her sex, no matter how justifiable. But she knew that in the stark realism of that encounter, this man had done only what he had to do. He was being true to his hire, protecting the interests of the man who paid his wages. He had been faced with the inexorable choice of kill or be killed.

Stagmire knew he was being judged. He spoke with a swift insight that deepened the color in her face.

"There are some things, Miss Hubbard, that a man does because he has to do them, not because he likes to." Saying this, he inclined his head slightly and went out.

Gib Dawson, a mite bewildered, looked up. "Youngster, what did you say to that boy? I didn't hear a word."

She showed him an uncertain smile. "Maybe

you weren't listening very closely, Mister Gib."

Outside, Stagmire went over to the corrals, began shaking out a rope.

Noyo came hurrying up. "No ride!" he objected.

"A little, Noyo," insisted Stagmire. "Not far, but just enough to start toughening up again."

Noyo, realizing the uselessness of arguing against the firmness in Stagmire's tone, shrugged. "I saddle for you. You go get gun. No ride even a little way without a gun."

So Stagmire went over to the bunkhouse for the weapon while Noyo caught and saddled for him. His side gave him only a slight twinge when he swung carefully up, and then he held his mount to a walk as he dropped down the slope to the river. He wasn't going anywhere in particular. It was just that he knew an edge of restlessness that he wanted to wear off.

Bill Vessels, Harley Jacks, and Buck Hare were off somewhere at the inland end of the valley, beginning a range count that Gib Dawson had decided on, so that he could get a more accurate estimate of his losses to Frank Lawrey's rustling activities. Tomorrow, thought Stagmire, he'd help them with that.

Following the run of the river, he went on down to the lower end of the valley where the pinched-in ridges formed the start of the cañon through which the Sotoyome River worked its way to the sea. His glance ranged somberly over

111

one timber slope. There was where guns had pounded and men had died.

His thoughts, ranging back to other days on other ranges, recalled comparable incidents there. No matter where a man rode, cattle were cattle and men were men, and their impulses for good or evil never changed. A rustler was a rustler, north, south, east, or west.

There were few Anchor cattle on this part of the range, just now. That was an angle that had been decided upon in a bunkhouse discussion. The farther back upvalley the cattle were kept, the more difficult it would be for the raiders to get at them. Bill Vessels and the others had done this job of driving during the two days Stagmire had spent in his blankets.

He rode on into the cañon and here the river foamed close by, serene for a distance in some long, quiet pool, then whipping swiftly over shallows and rock-ribbed riffles, where spray lifted and filled the air with its moist, cool breath. Here also was timber, close pressing, throwing its perpetual shadow, though thinning just enough in spots to let in a filtered sunlight. And where this occurred, masses of rhododendrons laid exotic bursts of colorful glory. Ferns grew lush and on the far cañon side where an ancient slide had gouged a small clearing, Indian paintbrush had taken over, laying a solid stain of scarlet, dusted with purple.

To Stagmire, used to the usual bleached aridity of other ranges, this sort of verdure was unique and stirring and he had reined in and was drinking up this wild beauty in silent appreciation when he heard the patter of hoofs on the trail behind him and he turned to see Stewart Hubbard riding up. She reined in beside him.

With a gesture of his hand, Stagmire indicated that scarlet stain yonder and a clump of rhododendrons closer by. "They're real enough, of course. But I find it hard to realize that."

"You should see the rhododendrons over on Mister Gib's Hester Creek property," she said. "That is a real fairyland."

Stagmire reached for his smoking. "Man," he observed, "can be a pretty crude customer. He tears a country like this apart . . . for his needs, so he claims. Sometimes I wonder if he's that important or worth the price?"

Faultless gray eyes studied him. "Strange words from a man in the saddle."

Stagmire nodded. "Perhaps. But you see beauty like this and then you remember all the ugliness that comes out of man's greed and selfishness and you can't fit the parts together. So it leaves you wondering."

"A cowboy philosopher," she jibed.

He spun a cigarette into shape, lit it, then swung his head and met her glance through the pale drift of tobacco smoke. "Hardly that. Just an ordinary mortal with eyes to see and enough brains to wonder." A faint smile touched his lips. "In this country beauty even comes riding down the trail."

Her naturally fresh color deepened. She started to answer, changed her mind, and lifted her horse to a run. Stagmire watched her out of sight. He stayed there, quiet, finishing his smoke. Then he rode back upriver.

Chapter Ten

They rode through a gloomy blanket of dense, dank fog, and into the teeth of a burly, roistering wind. Wade Stagmire and Bill Vessels. The outskirts of Castle City came spectrally up out of the driving, chill murk, and they walked their horses through the streets to a stop at the hitch rail in front of the Cattleman saloon.

Inside the Cattleman, though this was only midmorning, a couple of hanging lamps were glowing, fighting back the day's gloom. Dim as a far echo, the pound of foaming surf carried in, while closer and more raucous was the metallic drone of the saws in Jared Hubbard's mill.

Obie Chase, who owned the bar and tended it, put bottle and glasses before them and made a sober observation. "Been hearing things, Bill."

"Yeah?" said Vessels. "What?"

"Dead men in the timber. Two of them. Over on Gib Dawson's range."

"True enough," admitted Vessels dryly. "And if Harley Jacks and Buck Hare and I'd got there a little sooner, there probably would have been more than two. Damn' rustling vermin. Or didn't you hear that part of it, Obie?"

Obie shrugged. "Guessed as much. And my

private opinion, of course, is more power to you. But I'm only a fat bartender and small shakes. My opinion don't count. But there's talk."

"Who's making it?"

Obie shrugged again. "Who always makes it? Them with empty heads and big mouths. Just the same, it carries."

"Coming a little more to the point," put in Stagmire, "who's stirring up the talk?"

For a third time Obie twitched a fat, thickened shoulder. "If I had to make a guess, I'd say Frank Lawrey, with mebbe Ruel Tedrow adding his dime's worth here and there." The room was empty except for the three of them, so Obie made no attempt to keep his voice down. "I understand that Mitch Caraway has threatened to really rub the shine off anybody wearing spurs who stirs up any small sign of a ruckus inside the limits of town."

Bill Vessels turned his head and spat in huge contempt. "That hunk of rum-soaked blubber."

Even as Vessels spoke the door of the saloon swung and a bull of a man, wearing a ragged, dirty, blue-and-black checked Mackinaw, came in. A man thick all the way through, with a massive, bulging stomach. His face was broad and liquor-lined and his black eyes slightly protuberant. Where the flap of his Mackinaw sagged away, a badge showed, pinned to his gray wool shirt.

Sotto voce, Bill Vessels jeered: "The great man himself. Hi yah, Mitch."

The mockery in Vessels's tone and words sent thick color across Mitch Caraway's bloated features. He came up to the bar with measured ponderousness. His voice had the thickness of ocean fog and too much whiskey in it.

"Saw your horses out front. Figgered it a good time to warn you to go slow."

Bill Vessels widened his eyes in mock astonishment. "Go slow about what, Mitch? I don't savvy what you mean."

"You savvy . . . plenty," growled the marshal. "Trouble makin', that's what I mean."

Bill Vessels looked injured. "Me . . . make trouble? Why, Mitch, I never make trouble. You know I'm the most peaceful man in these parts. Why, I ain't sat in on the hanging of a cow thief since I don't know when."

Bill Vessels was spurring him and Caraway knew it. The marshal gave off a heavy, deepening anger. "Mebbe you helped bury a couple not too long ago," he blurted.

Vessels grinned with pure delight. "Why, Mitch, it's so good of you to admit you knew they were cow thieves. And don't you agree that all cow thieves should be buried, quick and deep?"

Caraway had blundered into this spot blindly and been tripped up. His face grew mottled. He tried to ignore Vessels while laying his protuberant glance directly on Wade Stagmire. "Seems you throw a ready gun, mister. Go slow at that kind of business. In these parts we don't take kindly to gunslingers. I ain't warnin' you a second time."

Before Stagmire could answer, Bill Vessels spoke with a vast innocence. "That's queer. I hadn't heard about it. When did they do it, Mitch?" Vessels emphasized his question with a thumb stabbed into the marshal's gross ribs.

Caraway flinched. "Do what?"

"Extend the limits of this town clear up the valley of the Sotoyome River."

Caraway moved a step away from Vessels, vastly irritated. "What the hell are you talkin' about, Vessels? Who said anything about the town limits bein' extended?"

"Then they didn't?" persisted Vessels. "Extend 'em, I mean?"

"Hell, no!" snapped the badgered marshal. "What gave you that crazy idea?"

Vessels's eyes crinkled maliciously. "You did. You were taking such big steps and absorbing so much territory." Abruptly Vessels was no longer smiling and his voice took on a hard bite. "If we want to bury a couple of cow thieves up along the Sotoyome, what's it to you, Mitch? Mebbe you got a dime's worth of authority inside the limits of Castle City, but not one damn' inch farther. So what are you throwing your weight around

118

about? Can't a couple of honest cowhands have a friendly drink together without you busting in full of bluster and bully-puss? Mitch, that gun ain't loaded, so don't try and point it at us."

It was like a balloon that had been punctured and was shrinking in size. Caraway began edging back toward the door. "You heard what I said," he blurted.

Bill Vessels's grin returned. "You ought to quit trying to walk that way, Mitch. You look funny as hell. With your foot in your mouth, I mean."

Caraway charged out of the place with a vehemence that threatened the door's hinges. Vessels spat again and looked at Wade Stagmire. "And they call that a town marshal."

Stagmire chuckled. "Bill, you're one cute son-of-a-gun. Never did see a bull led around by the nose so smooth and handy."

Vessels laughed soundlessly. "If somebody was to give Mitch Caraway one ounce of brains, then he'd have just one ounce. So far, nobody's been that generous."

Obie Chase had got a chuckle out of it, too. But now he sobered. "I hope you didn't miss the real point behind Mitch's little call, Bill?"

"I didn't. Ruel Tedrow's little chore boy, sent in to make a speech. Which means that while we mebbe ain't got 'em exactly worried, they're a mite irritated. Well, we might as well make the itch dig a little deeper. Let's have one more,

Wade, and then we'll go make our little call. I hope we find him in."

"Find who in?" asked Obie.

"Frank Lawrey. I understand he's taken to running most of his business from the office in his meat cooling plant. We'll have a look."

They left their horses at the hitch rail in front of the Cattleman and went along on foot, spur chains jangling and rowels clashing on the splintery board sidewalk. The wind stabbed chill fingers at them and occasional gusts were strong enough to force them to lean into it. The fog built tiny beads of moisture on their eyebrows and laid a salty wetness across their cheeks.

"Damn' stuff was a mite thicker a man would have to swim," growled Vessels.

A shadowy bulk on the far side of the street, Mitch Caraway watched them, marking their direction and finally guessing their destination. Satisfied of that, the marshal hurried ponderously off in the direction of Jared Hubbard's mill, his stride heavy and lunging.

Frank Lawrey's meat cooling plant stood well out toward the southern edge of the headland overlooking the lagoon at the mouth of the Sotoyome River. It was redwood-built, a square and squatty building with double walls packed with sawdust. There was a small office in one corner of it, heated by a cast-iron stove.

Frank Lawrey sat at his desk in the relaxed

comfort of shirt sleeves, under a hanging lamp's yellow glow, talking over items of business with his plant foreman, named Tanner. Lawrey looked up with swift irritation as the office door swung open and Wade Stagmire and Bill Vessels stepped in, bringing with them the raw, wet breath of wind and fog. For a moment Lawrey stared, then the irritation in his eyes faded to a guarded alertness. He leaned back in his chair and his hands dropped from sight below the desk top.

"You won't need a gun this time, Lawrey," said Bill Vessels harshly. "That may come later. Depends on whether you listen to reason."

Frank Lawrey sat silently for a time, studying them. On his part, Wade Stagmire had his good look at this man he'd heard so much about. Physically there was nothing particularly impressive about Lawrey. He was not a tall man and there was a sort of chubby roundness to him, both in body and face. His hair was sandy and closely cropped, his cheeks clean-shaven.

Either from long habit or some kind of muscular constriction, a slight squint to his eyes and an up-pulled corner of his mouth gave the impression that he was constantly on the verge of smiling in a musing sort of way, as though he were inwardly pleased about something. But this was a completely false impression, Stagmire concluded, once you caught the full gleam of the cold and calculating depth in his eyes.

Lawrey jerked his head. "That'll be all for now, Tanner."

The plant foreman nodded and went away. Lawrey took a cheroot from a desk drawer, lit it, and rolled it across his lips. "All right, Vessels. I'm listening."

Vessels said: "I'll let Wade Stagmire tell it, Lawrey. He's Gib Dawson's *segundo*."

Lawrey's glance settled steadily and coldly on Stagmire. "Well?"

Stagmire wiped the fog moisture from his hands, built a cigarette. Here, he realized, was a plenty cold proposition. He held Lawrey's glance across the flaring match that he touched to his cigarette, inhaled deeply, and let the smoke filter slowly over his lips.

"It's about cattle, mister. Gib Dawson's cattle. Two hundred head that you've lifted off Gib's range over a period of time. We aim to collect for those cattle. That's it."

It was hard to tell now whether Frank Lawrey's half smile was false or real. "Damn' broad statement, Stagmire. You got proof? I mean real proof, not just an opinion?"

"Proof good enough for us," said Stagmire.

"But not for me," rapped Lawrey, suddenly harsh. He brought both hands into sight, spread them on his desk, leaning forward. "For your information, I'm getting fed up completely with this rustling talk being thrown my way. For a long time now, Gib Dawson has been yapping such a song and he's yet to produce one smidgen of proof that wouldn't be laughed out of any law court."

"There's a couple of your riders buried in the timber at the lower end of Anchor range," retorted Stagmire. "What put 'em there? Why, being caught up with while they were trying to run off another jag of Anchor cattle."

"Who says they were my riders?" snapped Lawrey.

"I do, for one," put in Bill Vessels. "I oughta know. I helped bury them. By name they were Mogy Vidal and Rocky Gentry."

"I fired Vidal weeks ago," said Lawrey calmly. "The other one . . . you say his name was Gentry? Now it seems to me I recall a fellow by that name riding for Dawson. What's the answer to that?"

"The answer is that Gib Dawson fired Gentry some time back, along with two others, for selling him out to Price Mabry. Now I suppose you're going to try and say that Price Mabry ain't riding for you?" Vessels's tone was challenging and truculent.

Lawrey steepled his finger tips. "I don't know what you're talking about," he said smugly.

Bill Vessels began to growl, deep in his throat, like a badgered mastiff. Stagmire quieted him with a gesture. This fellow Lawrey was smooth and smart and shifty and he had a lot of answers.

There was, Stagmire realized, no chance at all of cornering him in this fashion and ragging him into any unwary admissions. Stagmire leaned across Lawrey's desk and a roughness flowed out of him that was far more penetrating and chill than the snorting wind outside.

"Something for you to think about, Lawrey. The slickest cow thief that ever lived was never quite smart enough to cover all his tracks all the time. Somewhere along the line they always slip up. You're no exception. I'm going to be looking for that slip-up on your part. When it comes, we won't bother with what a law court will have to say about it. And I won't worry too much about your hired hands. You'll be the merry little bandit who'll have to answer. You will . . . direct. That's a promise."

Lawrey tried to meet and hold Stagmire's glance, but the impact of it was too heavy and rough. So Lawrey puffed at his cheroot and, through the smoke of it, looked at the ceiling. And now Bill Vessels's simmering growl turned into words.

"While we're on the subject of who owes who for cows, there's the little matter of some eighty head that disappeared out of Wind Pike Valley. Losing that herd busted me and Harley Jacks and Buck Hare. You know what happened to that herd, and so do we. So, when the day of collecting comes around, me and Harley and

Buck aim to drag what's coming to us. Until that time, we're backing Gib Dawson to the limit. Everything Stagmire has said goes double for us."

"I still don't know what you're talking about," said Lawrey blandly.

Wade Stagmire saw by Bill Vessels's expression that it was in the raw-boned, reckless cowboy to reach across the desk, take Lawrey by the throat, and shake him until that smug mask slipped aside and revealed the rascality underneath. But that would have gained nothing and the time was not yet ripe for anything of the sort. For the seed had been sown and it was best to give it time to sprout. Stagmire threw a last barbed statement at Lawrey.

"It's always a mistake for any cow thief, big or little, to try and act proud, Lawrey. For no matter how he walks, he's still just a damned cow thief."

Here was the whiplash, and it stung. For even the most hardened thief did not like being catalogued so bluntly. Lawrey's false smile became more set and the flush of anger stained his cheeks. His voice thickened a little.

"Close the door when you go out."

That menacing growl began to build again in Bill Vessels, but Stagmire took him by the arm. "Come on, Bill. We've had our say. Lawrey knows exactly where we stand and how we see him. Let's get out of here."

Vessels, still simmering, reluctantly followed Stagmire out into the wind-driven fog.

For some time Frank Lawrey sat and stared at the door, and now that he was alone he let the mask slip aside while the taut and raging anger in him began to flow. He got rid of the worst of it in a torrent of almost inaudible cursing. Then he opened a desk drawer and brought out a gun in a shoulder holster. He buckled on the harness with quick, savage jerks, stood up, lifted his hat and Mackinaw from a wall peg, and donned them. He was starting for the door when Ruel Tedrow opened it and walked in.

Tedrow marked the look on Lawrey's face and spoke quickly. "Easy does it, Frank. I saw them leave. They were pretty rough?"

"Too damned rough," snapped Lawrey. "If they want a fight, they can damn' well have one."

"Easy," soothed Tedrow again. "Breaking into a big row just now wouldn't help us any, and it could raise the devil."

"This is our town," fumed Lawrey, "and no pair of ten-cent cowhands can come into it and push me around."

"Not yet," corrected Tedrow swiftly. "Not our town yet, Frank. Still Jared Hubbard's. And one word from him at this stage of the game could put us flat on our backs. Right now's the time to use our heads. Frank, we've made some mistakes and we can't afford to make any more."

126

Lawrey stamped around the office. "What mistakes?"

Tedrow swung the desk chair around, dropped into it, pushed his feet out, and leaned back. "Mainly," he frowned, "we've let the lure of a little immediate profit pull us off the trail of the big issue. We made a bad mistake when we made that raid on the herd belonging to Vessels, Hare, and Jacks."

"I can't see any mistake there," argued Lawrey. "Eighty head that Mabry and the boys got away with clean. Nice chunk of easy money there, man."

"Peanuts," scoffed Tedrow, "just peanuts compared to the big prize. And still a mistake, because it's put Vessels, Jacks, and Hare to riding for Gib Dawson again, which puts a lot of new strength into Dawson's hand just when we were getting him cut down to size. Frank, we had Dawson just about where we wanted him and now he's slipped away from us."

Lawrey chewed his cheroot, eyes pinched down. He nodded grudgingly. "I see what you mean. You got an angle there. But what's the rush? That Hester Creek timber of Dawson's has been there a long time. It's not going to dry up and blow away in the next few months. When we first decided to take it, we also agreed it was something we didn't have to rush."

"At that time, we didn't," said Tedrow. "It was

like money in the bank. It was our pot of gold to be dug up at our leisure. But something has happened that's hiked its value maybe as much as twenty-five percent. Think on this. I just came away from Jared Hubbard's office. Mitch Caraway was waiting outside for me and told me Stagmire and Vessels were headed down here. That only hurried me a little, for I was coming to see you anyhow."

The eagerness in Tedrow's tone focused Lawrey's glance more narrowly. "I'm listening."

"Those buyers from San Francisco who've been visiting with Hubbard . . . they represent the biggest accounts Hubbard has. And they've just got through laying it on the line. Seems there's another big building boom going on down in Frisco. And the buyers want at least thirty percent more lumber than we've ever been able to send them before . . . and they want it quick. They as much as told Hubbard that, if he couldn't fill the bill, they'd have to shift the bulk of their buying to one of the big outfits up around Eureka. You know what that means?"

"What does it mean?"

"It means plenty." Ruel Tedrow straightened in the chair, leaned forward, hands spread on his knees. "It means that Jared Hubbard's going to have to boost production and do it quick. It means extra shifts in the mill, more logging crews in the timber . . . and more timber. Most of all it means more timber, fat stands of it, easy to get at. Right now Hubbard hasn't got those stands of fat timber. He's got to go out and get them. And he's going to have to spend money, big money for such stumpage."

"That don't add up," protested Lawrey. "I know and you know that Jared Hubbard owns plenty of timber."

"Sure he does, Frank. But most of it is back-country timber, good stuff of course, but not too easy to get at. Lot of development work to do before that timber can be brought out to the mill, and such work takes time. Right now, time is the big factor. Come to think of it, the one mistake I've ever known Jared Hubbard to make in a business way is an entirely human one, but still a mistake. He's been cutting his more accessible timber stands first, and he has them pretty well used up. Now he's had this rush ultimatum thrown in his lap. He has to get out more timber than ever, and get it out quick, if he wants to hang on to his best accounts, which of course he does. So . . ."

"So, what?"

Tedrow leaned farther forward, his eyes glinting. "That stand of timber on Gib Dawson's Hester Creek range is exactly what Hubbard needs, and has to have. Quantity, quality, and comparatively easy to get at. Our pot of gold is right in sight now, Frank . . . if we got what it takes to move in. Jared Hubbard will pay a small fortune for that stumpage."

"Maybe," growled Lawrey. "But not to us, for we haven't got control of it yet. We haven't busted Gib Dawson, or pushed him out of the way. And the stubborn old buzzard won't sell that timber to Hubbard or you or me or anybody else . . . least of all to you or me. You know that. You're right in one thing. We should have worked him over a lot rougher a long time ago, busted him, and run him off his range. Then we'd have been in position to deal with Hubbard now."

"It's a condition that can be changed in a hurry," said Tedrow flatly.

"How?"

"By a few straight-aimed slugs put in the right places."

The cold intensity of Tedrow's words made Lawrey consider him in a long, narrow silence. There was a raw and hungry gleam in Tedrow's eyes, backed by the glitter of ruthless purpose. Lawrey stirred a trifle uneasily.

"Might take a lot of slugs, Ruel. It ain't only Dawson. It's Vessels and Jacks and Hare . . . and that new Anchor hand, Stagmire. Now there's a tough one, if I ever saw one. Cleaning the slate of that whole crowd won't be easy."

"Not easy, maybe, but it can be done. It's got to be done."

Lawrey mouthed his cheroot, gone cold now.

If he hesitated in any way over Ruel Tedrow's proposal of violence, it wasn't a matter of ethics. As far as Frank Lawrey was concerned, only fools worried about ethics. But at times, except when swayed by complete anger, there was a broad streak of sly caution in the man.

"We could finish ourselves with Hubbard completely if things got too raw, Ruel. Now there's nothing personal in this, you understand, but how about you and the girl, Stewart Hubbard? It's more or less general opinion that Jared Hubbard favors you as a husband for her. Which would mean that in time the whole Hubbard layout would go to you. We've kind of counted on that, with the Hester Creek timber as a side issue to all the rest. We get Hubbard with his roach up now, we could lose everything."

Mention of Stewart Hubbard deepened the color in Tedrow's florid face. Ruel Tedrow wasn't at all satisfied with Stewart Hubbard's manner of late. In the past ten days a distinct change had come over her, something quite alien to their former easy companionship. A sort of increasing remoteness on Stewart's part, a moving away, which could bode no good for some of his carefully calculated plans.

"Forget the girl," he ground out harshly. "I'm not gambling my future on the vagaries of any woman's mind. I'll be satisfied with my share of what Hubbard will pay for that Hester

Creek stumpage, and to hell with the rest."

Still Frank Lawrey wasn't satisfied. There were holes in Ruel Tedrow's abrupt plan that might not be easily filled. "Jared Hubbard can be a pretty sharp bargainer. Suppose he flatly refused to deal with us if we tried to hike the price? Again, Hubbard can be damn' stiff-necked about some things. Such as killing, for instance. He knows who owns that Hester Creek timber right now. Gib Dawson does. But Dawson turns up dead. And then we go to Hubbard offering the Hester Creek stumpage for sale. Hubbard's no fool. He'll tie the two things together. And then I doubt that he'd deal."

"He'll deal," insisted Tedrow. "He'll have to, or lose his shirt. I think I know Jared Hubbard's make-up better than anyone else alive . . . maybe better than he knows it himself. This company of his is his life, his god . . . his everything. He's built it up over the years, put blood and sweat into it. He's proud of it, wrapped up in it to the point that he lives it, night and day. I tell you, man, it's his religion. It's all he thinks about, all he cares about. And when the chips are down, he's not going to risk having it come apart in any way, just to satisfy some little twinge of conscience." Ruel Tedrow pushed to his feet, paced back and forth. "What's a small-time cowman to Jared Hubbard? You think he gives a thin damn whether Gib Dawson lives or dies? Particularly if it enables him to get his hands on a stand of timber that'll make his lumber company bigger and richer than ever? Would you, if you were in his place? Of course not. I tell you, Frank, human nature never changes. It's all a matter of values. If the price is big enough, there ain't a man alive who won't close his eyes at the right time. No, we can make this go, if we got guts enough. And when we get ready to lay our cards on the table, you leave the handling of Jared Hubbard to me. He'll pay . . . don't worry about that."

The lure of this thing was beginning to get hold of Frank Lawrey. Ever an unscrupulous man because of a consuming greed, the idea of a real chunk of money at one swift stroke fascinated him. Even the sly caution in him that told him that Ruel Tedrow's estimate of Jared Hubbard's ultimate virtue and honesty might be erroneously colored by Tedrow's own complete lack of such qualities began to weaken and fade before the bright glitter of gold.

"All right," he said. "Suppose we go at things like you say, Ruel. How we going to manage the rough end of the deal?"

Tedrow whirled on him. "Good God, man. What have you been paying Price Mabry big wages for all the time, if not for something like this?"

"Price is a tough hand," admitted Lawrey slowly. "But it's a heavy chore for him to handle alone."

"He won't have to go it alone. You got other riders. But Mabry can make it a good start by getting Stagmire and Vessels. Stagmire particularly. He's the one who's put new spine in Gib Dawson. With Stagmire and Vessels out of the way, the rest will be easy."

Lawrey searched for a match, nursed it alight, and held it to the cold end of his cheroot, sucking noisily, watching Tedrow. A heavy brutality had settled on Tedrow's features. A last twinge of caution made Lawrey speak carefully.

"Killing is always a messy business and has its risks, Ruel. You never know what it can start. People . . ."

Tedrow waved all argument aside. "I tell you this is lumber country and lumber is all that the people who count are interested in. Who's to give a damn if the word gets out that some back-country cowhands are smoked down? Just how much real ruckus were we able to scare up by talking around what happened to Vidal and Gentry in that raid that Stagmire busted up? None at all, man . . . none at all. Just so plenty of logs come in to the mill and plenty of lumber stacks up in the drying yards, that's all that counts in these parts."

Tedrow's certainty was convincing. Lawrey shrugged. "All right. I'll have a talk with Mabry. But he may want to bargain. How much will it be worth to us?"

"How much is that stand of Hester Creek timber worth? Figure from there, man."

Frank Lawrey drew a deep breath. "I think I can interest Mabry, Ruel, I think so." The usual blandness and that false half smile had settled over Lawrey's face again.

"Good enough," growled Tedrow. "We've made some money, you and I. But it's penny-ante stuff against what we can do now. There's no time to waste. The pressure is on Hubbard and that puts it on us. Turn Mabry loose and tell him to get it done."

Tedrow headed for the door, but paused as Lawrey spoke again. "One other thing, Ruel. Just how much stumpage is in that stand of timber on Hester Creek? Oh, I know it's big . . . but how big? When we reach the point of bargaining with Hubbard, we ought to have some fairly concrete figures to put in front of him."

"I've thought of that," Tedrow returned. "I've sent out word for Jack Lytell to report to me. Lytell is a drunken bum when there's a whiskey bottle around, but sober he's the sharpest timber cruiser I ever saw. I'm taking him out for a look at the Hester Creek stand, and, when he's done his figuring, his estimate won't be five percent in error. He's that good. Oh, we'll know what we're talking about, all right."

Chapter Eleven

In his favorite rocking chair, which Noyo had moved out onto the ranch house porch for him, Gib Dawson sat at ease and looked down across the bright green valley of the Sotoyome River with a serene contentment that had not been his for long, long months. For it was the way of a man, when the years had begun to pile their weight upon him, unconsciously to strive for and gratefully accept a certain fixed order and routine in his living days. Things were moving that way at Anchor now, and it was like healing balm to old Gib.

For so long had the old cattleman writhed over his physical inability to do anything concerning the way his holdings had weakened and slid away, what with Frank Lawrey's raiders cutting the heart out of his herd, and seeing only faithlessness among the very men he was paying wages to. Gib Dawson had been living just from day to day, seeing no hope of improvement in conditions on the morrow. And this state of affairs had pulled him all to pieces inside and filled him with a bleak despair.

And then, on the morning of what was probably his greatest disillusionment, a strange rider had come in out of the timber, a gaunt and hungry young rider who was branded a wanted man. But this rider had a certain direct something in his glance that Dawson had liked. So, in the dregs of his desperation, Dawson had hired Wade Stagmire. And this day, as he rocked gently back and forth, Gib Dawson rated that move as the wisest one he'd ever made in his life.

For with that act, a right-angled turn had come in the affairs of Anchor. Disintegration had stopped abruptly. Things were now stabilized again, on the mend, even on the upgrade. Stagmire had gone to town, and brought back three good, sound men to form a hard, tough core of a crew. He had shot apart an attempted raid on Anchor cattle. He'd thrown cold defiance into the teeth of the renegade opposition. The man was a fighter and he was smart. And faithful. So it was that the affairs of Anchor were once more grooved and definite and smooth-working.

All these were facts that old Gib turned over in his mind as he puffed his pipe and rocked his chair and surveyed this little valley that was his chosen spot in the world. The day before, Gib had sent Noyo into Castle City with a written message, and now Gib was watching the river trail for an answer to that message. It came finally in the form of a bouncy little man with ruddy cheeks and a mane of electric, silvered hair, riding a sedately jogging black mare.

The little man pulled in beside the corrals, dismounted, lifted down a briefcase tied to his saddle horn, flexed his legs, and rubbed the inside of his thighs with a careful hand. He limped a little as he came up to the porch.

"Dog-gone you, Gib!" he yelled. "You want to cripple me up, making me ride 'way out here? I'm all stove up. Come tomorrow morning I won't be able to get out of bed." But a cheerful grin took all the sting out of the complaint.

Gib Dawson chuckled. "Good for you, Henry. Stir up that lazy liver of yours. Appreciate your coming, of course, but I can't feel sorry for you just because you've discovered a muscle or two you'd forgot you had."

They shook hands.

"Couldn't dim my ears to the call of an old friend," said Henry Carroll, lawyer. "And, saddle-galled or not, I'm really enjoying this. Good excuse to get out of that cussed fog for a time. We've had two solid weeks of it in town, and that can get damned monotonous, besides bleaching out a man's disposition as well as his hide. This sunshine feels almighty good to me."

There was a round-backed chair by the door and the lawyer pulled this out beside Dawson and settled into it with a sigh. "When a man lets himself grow to fit a chair, then he sure doesn't fit a saddle worth a whoop. That's me. From the hips down I'm just not built to curve around

139

horseflesh. Now then, what's this call to duty all about?"

Dawson reloaded his pipe before answering. He cleared his throat. "It came to me the other day that I wasn't growing any younger, Henry. So I figure to have you draw me up a will. There's something else I want you to look into, too. But first things first, which is the will."

The lawyer studied the gaunt old cattleman for a swift and searching moment. "You look just as ornery and tough to me as you did ten years ago, Gib. Maybe a little more grizzled around the edges, but still bright-eyed and bushy-tailed. And tough as saddle leather. Don't tell me you got one of these here premonitions?"

Dawson shook his head. "Nope, nothing like that, Henry. But I ain't overlooking the percentage odds, either. So, we draw up that will."

Henry Carroll reached for his briefcase. "Who's to be the beneficiary, Gib? I didn't know that you had any kin?"

"Haven't," was the terse answer. "In this will I'm namin' Wade Stagmire."

The lawyer stared. "New one to me. Never heard the name before."

"I know," Dawson responded. "But I have. He's my top hand. There's a little story."

And then Dawson told it. "Anchor and me were falling apart the day that boy came riding in," he ended. "I was just an old worn-out *hombre*, being slow but certain busted, with the ranch slipping away from me. Wade stopped all that. He took hold like a champion and pulled things through. He's all man. And I'm fonder of him than any man I ever knew. So, when I'm gone, I want everything I own to go to Wade Stagmire. Everything. Lock, stock and barrel. Write that down, Henry?"

"Does this Stagmire have any idea that you're doing this, Gib?" Carroll asked.

Dawson shook his grizzled head. "Not the slightest. If he did, he'd kick like hell, being the sort of lad he is." Dawson paused, taking a deep drag at his pipe. He added slowly: "If it should happen, and I'm praying the Lord it never will, but if it should come about that something happened to Wade, times being pretty uncertain, then I want everything to go to Stewart Hubbard."

Henry Carroll gave another start of surprise. "As flat as that, Gib? No conditions?"

"Nary a single damn' condition, Henry. Write it down."

So it was written and Gib Dawson signed it, and Carroll witnessed it and dated it. Gib Dawson gave a sigh of satisfaction. "Now that's done, I feel better. You take that and lock it in your safe, Henry. You'll know what to do about it when the time comes."

Carroll stirred uneasily. "Don't talk like that,

Gib. You got a lot of good years in you yet, old settler."

Dawson shrugged. "Mebbe. Hope so. I got a few things I'd sure like to see become real. But any man's a fool to take too much for granted."

The lawyer tucked the will carefully away in his briefcase. "You mentioned another angle, Gib, that you wanted me to look into. What is it?"

The cattleman turned his head and looked keenly at Carroll. "This ain't to go an inch past your lips, Henry. At least, not until you got all the answers I hope you get. A damn' good man's whole future can be riding on this."

Carroll settled deeper into his chair. "If you weren't my good friend, I'd yank your ears back for even suggesting I didn't know how to respect a confidence, Gib. Go ahead and talk. I'm listening."

Gib Dawson told of the Wanted poster that Wade Stagmire had shown him the day he first arrived at Anchor. "Now then, Henry," went on the cattleman, "I think you'll have to agree that nothing could have proven better how straight up and down that boy plays the game. He didn't have to show me that dodger. He didn't have to say a word about it and I'd never have been any the wiser. But when I offered him a job, he'd not take it until he'd shown me the dodger and left it up to me to decide. Right then and there I knew I could trust that boy plumb to hell and back. You agree?"

The lawyer nodded gravely. "It certainly couldn't be called a mark against him." Carroll got out a cigar. "Not a pleasant charge for a man to have hanging over him, though."

"That's where you come in, Henry. Wade's young, got all his life ahead of him. It ain't right that he have that cloud always at his shoulder. Me, I'm convinced complete that he told me the exact truth as to what happened and how it happened. Yeah, he killed a man . . . this Dodd Evans. But no clearer case of self-defense ever took place. So that's what I want you to do, Henry. It's to get the record cleared, get self-defense established, the murder charge against Wade squashed complete, and that Evans family put where they belong. Mebbe it would be smart for you to take a trip into that central valley country to get the job done. I'll be glad to pay your expenses and whatever fee you figger it's worth."

The lawyer was silently thoughtful for some little time. Then he nodded. "That would be the best and quickest way . . . that I get right on the ground. For that matter, I think I'll enjoy the trip. It's been a long time since I saw any other part of the country than this. You say the name of the fellow Stagmire had to kill was Evans . . . Dodd Evans?"

"That's right." Then Gib went on to give the lawyer all the other data that he recalled from the dodger, which Carroll took down in rapid notes, murmuring to himself. "Place . . . River Junction. Sheriff . . . Cass Roberts."

These notes Carroll also stowed carefully away in his briefcase. Then he leaned back and puffed his cigar. "Show me a family like this Evans layout, Gib . . . a family that's big and powerful and proud to the extent that they think the law was made to apply to everybody but themselves . . . and I'll show you a family with plenty of skeletons in the closet."

"That," agreed Gib Dawson, "was just about my thought, Henry. It's an angle for you to work on."

"It's an angle I intend to work on," declared the lawyer. "With a family like that, a lot of their bully-puss tactics are calculated to cover up things they're ashamed of. Now if I can't drag some of those skeletons out into the open, then my name isn't Henry Carroll. And when I begin to rattle bones, I'll bet that Evans tribe will be only too glad to forgive and forget. Gib, we'll squelch this charge against Wade Stagmire. So much for business. Now for pleasure. What's for dinner? As I remember, Noyo can sure swing a mean skillet."

Chapter Twelve

Some of them had been old before the first white man ever set foot on the western hemisphere, before any man ever dreamed such a land existed. To them, days were like ticks of a clock, years minute segments of time. They marched with the centuries. From massive base to incredibly lofty tip far up in the clean, free heavens, all was serene, strong, tapered grace and beauty. They had strength that laughed at the wildest storm, and foot thick bark that fire could not daunt. Their lifeblood held an acid that destroyed insects that otherwise might destroy them. Their will to live lifted them above all of Nature's ordinary forms of decay and corruption. Only man could despoil them. They were the redwoods.

On the long running flats of Hester Creek they marched in seemingly endless aisles of cathedral silence and dignity. Their size and their numbers and their brooding presence dwarfed all lesser life so that the world held to a humble hush beneath them. They drank deep of ocean's fog and winter's drenching rains, but they loved to drowse in the sunlight, too, and then they would relent and let shafts of that light glimmer down through them in lances of gold, to heighten the massed glory of rhododendrons and the green, smooth-swept grace of giant ferns. They were the redwoods.

Men moved under them. Two men. Ruel Tedrow and Jack Lytell. Minute creatures, plotting destruction. Two who would reduce all this to that crass denominator that some men called wealth. They saw none of the beauty, sensed none of the spell of age and permanency. They judged these great trees by one measurement alone. How many board feet when the loggers had finished and the mill saws had whined, and the skies were empty and lonely, and remained only the intangible ghosts of what had once been.

Tedrow and Lytell had ridden out some distance from Castle City along the Sotoyome River trail, then cut back up onto the north ridge, crossed it, and dropped down to the western beginning of the Hester Creek flats. There they had left their horses and moved into the stand of redwoods on foot. They spoke seldom. Jack Lytell knew what Tedrow wanted and he set about this business immediately, with tape and notebook and pencil.

He was a man of medium size, prematurely gray, with a rather fine face that had been punished and scarred with deep lines by a weakness he could not control, an over-fondness for whiskey. But it was as Ruel Tedrow had told Frank Lawrey. Sober, there was no more shrewd and able timber cruiser than Jack Lytell.

Lytell made one remark before he set to work.

"Never saw a fatter stand. Fairly close in, too . . . and easy to get at."

"All of which I damn' well know," answered Tedrow brusquely. "Get at the job."

Lytell selected an average tree here and there, measured, calculated, estimated, figured in his notebook, set down totals. He estimated area, density, moved on. Finished with one flat, they sought their horses and rode on to the next.

This was the one kind of work Jack Lytell knew and knew well. It revived in him the burned-out coals of an interest that had once been a passion, back in the days of his youth when a man's dreams could be great and fine and the world was clean and uncorroded in his eyes. A faint flush showed in Lytell's gaunt cheeks and his faded eyes brightened. He spoke again.

"I always understood that this Hester Creek timber belonged to that cattleman, Gib Dawson. You got a deal figured out with him, Tedrow?"

Tedrow's answer was harsh, the old arrogance hardening his face. "I didn't bring you here to ask questions, Lytell. So, don't. Get what I brought you here to get, then forget it . . . forget all of it." Then, because he was the kind of man he was, Tedrow had to add: "The whiskey will help you do that."

Lytell flushed. After that he did not speak any more.

Half an hour later, in a world where there

had been no movement beyond their own, they glimpsed movement. Cattle—three or four of them, breaking through the ferns, heading for the creek to drink. And right after that a rider, a big, red-headed cowboy, riding at a walk, following the sign left by the cattle.

Ruel Tedrow rapped out a low-toned order to Jack Lytell. "Quick! Get out of sight! Some damn' fool would have to ride in . . . !"

Tedrow's mistake lay in the very swiftness with which he moved to put the bulk of a tree between himself and Harley Jacks. Had Tedrow and Lytell remained stockstill in their tracks, the chances were strong that Harley wouldn't have seen them, for Harley's attention was all on locating these few cows he'd been trailing, with the purpose of again hazing the critters back up across the ridge to the open range of Gib Dawson's valley.

But nothing alerts the casual eye like glimpsing some quick, startled move. From the corner of his eye, Harley caught that move, and his head swung and he stared, and then he reined his horse that way and closed in quickly on Ruel Tedrow and Jack Lytell. Realizing that further attempt at concealment was not only useless but must seem foolish, Tedrow stood his ground, ripping out a low-toned order to his companion.

"Keep your mouth shut. I'll do the talking."

Harley Jacks recognized Tedrow, but could not remember ever having seen Tedrow's companion before. However, he had seen others like him, and, while there was a lot Harley did not know about lumbering, he did recognize a timber cruiser at work when he saw one. Easy-going, good-natured Harley's glance turned a little cold as he reined in and looked this pair over. He spoke bluntly.

"What's the idea, Tedrow?"

Ruel Tedrow had on his red-and-black checked Mackinaw. He folded his arms casually, a move that put his right hand in a position to dart instantly under the flap of the Mackinaw toward his left armpit. A lot of things were racing through Ruel Tedrow's mind at the moment, but he kept his eyes veiled and his face expressionless.

"I don't understand your question, cowboy. What's the idea of . . . what?"

Harley's jaw took on a slight jut. "I'll make it plainer. What's the idea of cruising timber that belongs to Gib Dawson?"

Ruel Tedrow's look of simulated astonishment was not very convincing. "Man, you're mistaken. This isn't Gib Dawson's range. This is . . ."

"The hell it's not Dawson's range," cut in Harley bleakly. "You know damned well it is, and so do I. And knowing you, and knowing old Gib, I'm plenty certain he never gave you any authority to prowl his land and cruise his timber. So now I'm telling you to get off, and stay off! What with the trouble we've had with Frank

Lawrey and his gang, and knowing how thick you and Lawrey are, you're just not the right breed of cat that Anchor wants prowling around. So, git! Light a shuck!"

Jack Lytell was vastly uneasy and plainly only too anxious to move on and get out. There was no real fiber of any kind left in Jack Lytell. All the courage he had once owned had long since been burned out of him by alcohol. He looked at Harley Jacks, looked at Ruel Tedrow, then drifted away a few steps.

Ruel Tedrow's mind was racing frantically. He'd never expected to meet up with anyone, here along the Hester Creek flats. And such a meeting was the last thing in the world that he wanted. For complete secrecy at this stage of the game that he and Frank Lawrey were playing was very important. Least of all, if he had to meet up with someone, did Tedrow want that someone to be a person such as Harley Jacks, an Anchor rider, who would certainly take the news of the meeting to Gib Dawson. That could be disastrous. For Gib Dawson, on hearing that Ruel Tedrow had been found cruising timber on Hester Creek, would be almost certain to draw all manner of deductions. Dawson's natural assumption would be that Jared Hubbard had ordered this cruising move, in which case Dawson might, and probably would, go straight to Hubbard and demand an explanation.

Out of such a situation, and because of Hubbard's need of easily accessible and extensive, rich stumpage such as this stand, might come a direct timber deal between Dawson and Hubbard, and if this happened, then where would be his own and Frank Lawrey's fine and ambitious plans? Also, even if no deal came up between Dawson and Hubbard, of a certainty Jared Hubbard would demand an explanation of such cruising activity and what answer could Tedrow give him that wouldn't expose the whole hand he and Lawrey were playing?

These and other questions of similar vein sped through Ruel Tedrow's mind like flashes of light. And the answers that jumped back at him began to stampede him, rushing him into a conclusion that put little flecks of crimson burning deep in his eyes, while brushing his face with certain brutishness, in which slyness and cunning and ruthlessness were combined. He knew what he had to do, what he was going to do. He shrugged and turned away.

"If I'm wrong in figuring out where Dawson's line runs, why I'm wrong. I don't want trouble with anyone. We'll get out. Come on, Jack."

All the time he was speaking and with the turn of his burly body hiding what he was about, Ruel Tedrow's right hand was sliding inside his Mackinaw toward his left shoulder. His fingers closed about the butt of the gun slung there in

151

a shoulder holster. And once he had the weapon gripped solidly and sure, with an explosive spurt of action Tedrow came whirling back again.

Had Harley Jacks known this fellow Ruel Tedrow a little better, he would not have missed the sullen fire that had kindled in Tedrow's eyes, nor the sly brute shadow that swept Tedrow's face. Particularly would the false mildness of Tedrow's tone have been high warning to him as the man turned away. But Harley, after delivering his blunt ultimatum for Tedrow and his companion to move on and get off Anchor property, and seeing the pair of them about to comply, had relaxed a little from the first high alertness that had held him. Now, with Tedrow spinning back toward him so explosively fast, and with a gun in his fist, Harley tried desperately to recover and catch up. He almost made it, but not quite. Harley had his own gun clear of the leather and beginning to lift, when Tedrow's weapon stabbed at him and blasted flame and report.

The big, red-headed, happy-go-lucky cowboy reeled in his saddle under the impact of the wicked blow that smashed him in the middle of his chest. He recovered slightly and lunged half forward again, blindly trying to get his gun up and level. But again Tedrow's gun blasted and again that merciless force hammered into Harley, and now the world went dark and everything real and tangible ran away from him. There was nothing but everlasting darkness left to Harley Jacks now, and into it he plunged headlong, and he never knew the shock as the earth took him— the faithful, patient, eternal earth. . . .

The massed redwoods took in the reports of Ruel Tedrow's weapon, smothered them to puniness, swallowed them up. A complete and pitying silence came down. It was broken by the hard, unbelieving gasp that burst from Jack Lytell. "Great God, man! You killed him! He's dead. Why . . . ?"

Ruel Tedrow's reeking gun turned toward Jack Lytell, and in the twisted ferocity on Tedrow's face showed the half-formed intention to kill again, and so wipe out all witnesses. Lytell recognized the thought and cringed before it.

"Man, man!" he cried. "Don't . . . !"

Tedrow didn't, for cold caution rang a small bell at the back of his mind. Men had seen him ride out of Castle City with Jack Lytell. These men would have no idea of where or why they were riding, but they would remember having seen the pair go off together. And if Ruel Tedrow came back alone, while Jack Lytell never came back . . .

Tedrow holstered his gun, but the ugly fury in him still showed in his face. He stared for a long moment at the huddled, lifeless figure of Harley Jacks, and then he turned and bent the full threat of his glance on the shaking, stupefied

Jack Lytell. "Yeah," he rapped harshly, "I killed him. The damned, blundering fool! I killed him because there was no other answer. It's an answer, Lytell, that needn't concern you at all. It better not concern you. If it ever does, then you'll be where he is . . . quick! Understand? You're to forget this. It never happened. You never saw or heard anything. We weren't here at all. We rode out of town to look over some timber miles away from Hester Creek. That's all. That's every bit of it. Understand?"

Jack Lytell nodded, cringing. His mouth hung, open and loose. He fumbled with his gear, his hands shaking. He dropped his notebook and pencil, stooped and recovered the notebook, but forgot the pencil. He was on the verge of complete, terrified collapse. There was nothing left in this weak and whiskey-punished man.

Ruel Tedrow's lips curled with contempt and then Tedrow ignored Lytell, his glance going back again to Harley Jacks. Tedrow drove his mind back into logical channels. There lay a dead man, a man he had just killed. What to do about it? Harley Jacks would certainly be missed and other Anchor riders would search for him. In time he would be found, but how soon? Perhaps not for days, even weeks or months. In which case the trail would be so cold no man could follow it. Tedrow's first thought that he would have to do something with the body of Harley

Jacks, to try and hide it somewhere, now left him. For, come to think of it, there were plenty of other conditions that could hide the real trail and confuse men's minds. There had been that other shoot-out, over at the lower end of the Sotoyome River Valley, when that fellow Wade Stagmire had broken up a rustling raid and finished two of Frank Lawrey's riders. Well, couldn't it be the natural conclusion of those who might find Harley Jacks that this was the result of some like affair? Even if Harley Jacks was found within a matter of hours, that would be the way men would think. A gleam of satisfaction came into Ruel Tedrow's cold eyes. Let Harley Jacks lay just as he was. Let his friends hunt for him and find him. Let them guess what they would. What chance had they of guessing the truth?

Tedrow turned and looked at Jack Lytell once more. Lytell was leaning against a tree, head down, staring at nothing. Here was a dangerous witness all right, but this was not the time to get rid of that witness. That time could come later, after those who had seen him and Lytell ride out of Castle City together had the chance to see them ride back in again. Tedrow knew growing satisfaction at the way his mind was working. Cool, now—cool and clear. Not being stampeded into making some vital mistake. But calculating every risk, every possibility, leaving no stupid loopholes. He stepped over to Lytell, grabbed him by the arm, gave him a shake. "Pull yourself together, man." His tone was almost mild. "Who really gives a damn about some two-bit cowhand getting rocked off? Nobody who counts. You and me, we're the only ones who know and we're not telling. We're going back to town, Jack. I'll see that you have a couple of bottles. And once you get outside of them, you won't care. Only, keep your mouth shut." Tedrow's tone grew brittle and cold again. "You keep your mouth shut, or it'll be shut forever. Understand?"

Jack Lytell wagged his head weakly up and down. He understood, all right. His flesh crawled under Tedrow's heavy hand.

So they went away, slipping through the still and brooding majesty of these great trees and soon they were out of sight and gone. Left was only Harley Jacks, a small speck of crumpled lifelessness under all this towering age. Just Harley Jacks and his horse, hanging nervously about. And nearby, at the base of a towering forest giant, a small sliver of graphite and yellow painted wood. A pencil—the pencil that Jack Lytell, in his terror and weakness, had dropped and not recovered. A shaft of sunlight touched it, heightening its betraying color.

Chapter Thirteen

These peaceful days that had settled over the Sotoyome River Valley were as welcome to Wade Stagmire as they were to Gib Dawson. But they did not deceive him. They could represent the calm before the storm. Throwing the rawhide directly into the teeth of Frank Lawrey would undoubtedly give the man some pause, but it was highly doubtful that it would stop him altogether. So, the smart thing to do, as Stagmire saw it, was not to relax vigilance in any way at all. In one way it rasped a man's nerves to sweat out the days, waiting for trouble to strike. In another it was a vast relief to gain the time to steady down and build the fences of his security a little higher with each passing hour.

The lower end of the valley being the danger spot in so far as future raids by Lawrey were concerned, Stagmire had laid out a plan to equalize the grazing. Every morning, along with Bill Vessels, Harley Jacks, and Buck Hare, he would work a part of the herd down across these lower stretches to feed, guard them through the day, and then, with evening coming on, drift the cattle farther up the valley again where it would be harder for Lawrey to get at them. There was a lot of monotony in this maneuver, but it was sound. So they kept to it.

Throughout the hours that the cattle grazed the lower end of the valley, two would guard while the other two would ride patrol of the higher limits of the range. This day Harley Jacks and Buck Hare had drawn that chore, while Stagmire and Vessels watched the cattle. It was in Bill Vessels to growl at comparative inactivity and he was grumbling now.

"If Lawrey's going to take another cut at us, I wish he'd turn his wolf loose. I'm beginning to think, Wade, that us laying cold turkey in front of him has scared him off for good."

"I'd like to agree with you, Bill." Stagmire shrugged. "Sure save us a lot of time and energy. And while you could be right, I doubt it. We'll just have to wait and see and sweat it out."

So this one, like other days, they sweated out through the long slow hours. And finally there was a sunset that made the western sky all ablaze with scarlet and gold as the sun dipped beyond the ocean's distant fog banks. After that came a soft blue twilight that slowly filled the little valley of the Sotoyome. Through this peaceful dusk, Stagmire and Bill Vessels drifted Anchor cattle from the dangerous lower end of the valley up to the safer central and more inland areas. Buck Hare came jogging out of the forming shadows to help them. He picked up a drifting point of cattle, pushed them back among their fellows, then dropped in beside Stagmire.

"Where's Harley?" Stagmire asked.

Buck Hare looked around. "Thought he'd be down here with you and Bill."

Stagmire shook his head. "Haven't seen him since you and him headed out on patrol this morning, Buck."

Buck stood in his stirrups, took another look across the dusk. "That's damn' funny," he said slowly. "Thought sure he'd be here. Last I saw of him he was patrolling that north ridge. I figured, when he didn't show up again, that he'd probably bumped into you and you'd kept him here for some reason."

A hundred yards to their left, Bill Vessels was swinging an idle rope end, mildly cussing some reluctant and slow-moving critters. Buck rode over to him.

"You seen anything of Harley, Bill?"

"Not a damn' thing, Buck. Figgered he was with you."

Buck explained about the north ridge and Vessels said: "He probably just found himself a good place in the sun and stuck there. And then, with evening coming on, he probably figgered we wouldn't need him to drift these cows . . . which we don't . . . and so he headed straight back to headquarters."

This was logical and they let it go at that,

but when they had the cattle far enough back up the valley and had left them in the dark's first fullness and jogged on up to headquarters, Harley's saddle was not on the pole, his horse was not in the corral, nor was Harley anywhere around. Uneasiness caught at them and grew all the time they were washing up and eating supper. Buck Hare was particularly on edge, for he and Harley Jacks had been especially close in their companionship. Buck built an after-supper cigarette, sucked on it jerkily, then spun the butt aside. His words ran harshly.

"Harley's a full-grown man and knows his way around. But broncos have fallen before this and cracked up a rider. Harley may be laying out somewhere with a broken leg or something of the sort. Wade, I'm saddling and taking a little ride."

"That makes three of us," said Stagmire. "Come on, Bill."

They rode until midnight. They combed the north ridge from top to bottom and for all its long length. They sent a hundred calls through the night's blackness. They got no answer and they found nothing. They rode back to headquarters and turned in, silent and definitely worried now.

They were at breakfast the next morning when Gib Dawson came stumping in. "You boys did some riding last night," he said shrewdly. "Heard you leave and heard you come back. Something's wrong. What is it?"

His face was somber as they told him and his voice rang harshly. "Let everything else slide. Find Harley. Noyo, you go with them. I don't like this . . . I don't like it at all."

They were out on that north ridge again by sunup. They started at the point where Harley and Buck Hare had split up for yesterday's patrol. "He headed that way," said Buck, pointing west.

Noyo took the lead, following the tracks of Harley's horse. In some places, where it stuck to well-cut cattle trails, it was easy to follow. But there were spots where Harley had cut up or down a slope from one meandering trail to another where it was more difficult. And then, along some of the trails, wandering cattle had already covered much of the sign. But Noyo, his broad, brown face stoic and expressionless, his black eyes intent, would swing from his saddle in such places and prowl carefully afoot. And at no time was he seriously at fault. Finally, near that north ridge's highest point, Noyo stopped and swung an arm.

"Harley cross here, go that way. Down to Hester Creek. Few cattle cross here and Harley go after them."

They topped the rim and dropped down into the timber, where morning's sunlight was blotted out and a chill half light took over. Here, in the soft forest mold, the cattle sign and that of Harley's horse were deeply gouged and easy to follow.

They reached the Hester Creek flats where the giant, close-ranked redwoods held their silent, brooding court and Wade Stagmire found himself wondering bleakly how they could hope to find anything as insignificant as a man among these towering, majestic patriarchs?

They found Harley's horse first, or, rather, the animal found them, whickering its shrill relief, moving forlornly up to them with dragging reins. Stagmire looked at Buck Hare. Buck's face was expressionless, woodenly set, except for his eyes. There, Stagmire saw a weary dread.

They left it up to Noyo to work out. Noyo had dismounted again and was casting here and there, backtracking the tangled wanderings of Harley's horse. And so, finally, there was Harley.

He lay exactly as he had fallen from his saddle, his hat off, his red hair and his clothes moist from night's chill mists and the lifting dampness of the forest floor. His gun, unfired, lay beside him.

They dismounted and stood there, at a momentary loss. Over the growing tension of the past hours, all of them had come to expect something like this, for only something of the sort was the logical answer to Harley's absence. Yet, faced with actuality, the last thread of clinging hope completely severed, they were shocked and numbed and stupid.

It was Buck Hare who moved first. Buck picked

up Harley's gun, wiped it off carefully with a bandanna handkerchief, checked the cylinder full of unfired cartridges. Buck moved with an almost mechanical stiffness as he did this, like a man dazed from some savage blow. He took his own gun from the holster, put it in his saddlebags. He dropped Harley's gun into the empty holster at his hip. Then he whirled on Noyo with a sudden, bursting fierceness.

"All right, damn it . . . all right! Get at it. Let's have the rest of the trail. Harley didn't have a chance to use this gun, but I god damn well am going to have my chance. Come on . . . come on! The damn' whelps who did this must have left a trail leading somewhere and I'm going to follow it to the end if it takes the rest of my life. Get at it!"

Noyo's black eyes were gentle as he glanced at Buck. He did not resent this wild harshness, for he understood exactly how Buck felt. He felt that way himself, as they all did. Ferociously hungry for something real to hit at, to smash and destroy. All tied up inside with a mocking frustration. For there wasn't a thing to go on except a few faintly vague markings on the forest floor which only Noyo could make out at all, and these with little enough meaning.

Noyo did his best. He circled again and again. He drifted away through the massed columns of the trees until he was hidden completely, while Wade Stagmire and the rest waited with grinding impatience. Noyo came back to them again, prowling, searching intently. Nearby, he gave a soft exclamation, bent, and scooped up something, which he examined closely, and then held it out to Stagmire. It was a pencil, a yellow pencil, only a little used.

The others crowded around, looked at the pencil as Stagmire turned it over and over in his hand. "What," burst out Bill Vessels, "the devil does that mean? Now who the devil . . . ?"

Stagmire shook his head, putting the pencil carefully away. "No answer yet, Bill. But it might mean something. Well, Noyo . . . any other clues?"

Noyo jerked his head toward the west. "I think they go that way. Who shot Harley must have been on foot." Noyo dug up a gout of forest mold with a jabbing boot toe. "In this horses or cattle leave sign easy to follow. But a man on foot, no. Not enough for Noyo to be sure."

"But they must have had horses somewhere," rapped Buck Hare, his voice ragged. "Find their horse sign!"

Noyo shrugged, waved an arm in a wide circle. "Where to look? Mebbe they leave their horses a mile, two miles from here. Noyo willing to try, but don't think he can do much good."

"Noyo's right, Buck," said Stagmire quietly. "In this timber a man might look for a week for

164

the spot where they left their horses, and still not find the place."

"Those cows that drifted down here," said Bill Vessels. "Harley was definitely following them. Where did the damn' critters go?"

"Cows come here and drink, then go back upslope to open side of ridge again," explained Noyo.

"But Harley wasn't shot for nothing," raged Buck Hare. "He must've bumped into some kind of damn' shady business."

"No question about that," agreed Stagmire. "But I've got a feeling that business had nothing to do with cattle this time, Buck. We can't do a lick of good here, so we're taking Harley out . . . now."

It was midmorning by the time they rode in at Anchor headquarters again. Stewart Hubbard's fine-looking sorrel mount was standing tied to the corral fence. As they drew to a halt in front of the bunkhouse, Gib Dawson and Stewart Hubbard came out on the ranch house porch. Wade Stagmire went over to them, his face gravely quiet.

Gib Dawson, looking old and tired as he viewed the figure tied on Harley's horse, cleared his throat huskily. "You found him, of course . . . and he was dead?"

"That's right," Stagmire told him. "Shot . . . twice. Noyo did his best to work out some kind of a trail, but all he could come up with was . . . this."

Stagmire produced the pencil Noyo had found, held it out. Gib Dawson took it, turned it over in his fingers. "Where?" he rapped.

"Down in the big timber on the Hester Creek flats," Stagmire explained. "The readable sign showed that three or four head of our cattle drifted over the ridge crest and on down to Hester Creek, probably to drink. Apparently Harley picked up that sign, followed it down to haze the cattle back to the valley range. And down there he bumped into something that somebody was willing to shoot a man to cover up."

"Some more of Frank Lawrey's deviltry!" burst out Dawson. "Out to lift some more of our cows. . . ."

Stagmire shook his head. "Don't think so, Gib. Not that particular jag of them that Harley was after. For those cows came back across the ridge again."

"Mebbe they lost their nerve after gunning Harley," persisted the old cattleman. "Mebbe they figgered some other of my boys would have heard the shooting and would ride in to investigate?"

"That could be," said Stagmire. "But I doubt it. In that deep timber the sound of a shot wouldn't carry two hundred yards. No, I don't think it was cattle trouble this time."

Stewart Hubbard had not said a word. She had

166

stared, pale of face and stricken of eye, at the figure of Harley Jacks, tied across his saddle. Now she was staring at the pencil that Gib Dawson was mechanically turning over and over in his fingers. And her breath came out of her in a tragic little gasp.

"That pencil, Mister Gib . . . it's the same brand that's used in all of Uncle Jared's offices by the clerks and bookkeepers . . . by all the company employees who have need of a pencil in their work. And I don't. . . ."

"Whoa, lass . . . whoa," cut in Dawson gently. "That doesn't mean a thing. Likely enough it's a common brand of pencil. I bet Sam Alexander sells plenty of them right out of his Castle City store. Anybody could have bought this one. Then again, lots of folks lose pencils that other folks find and use. So, just because Noyo found this one along Hester Creek, it doesn't necessarily mean a thing."

Wade Stagmire realized what the old cattleman had in mind, which was to comfort this girl's quick fears. So he helped Dawson out. His glance touched her face and he said: "It's mighty rough on you, Miss Hubbard, to have to bump into this sort of thing just about every time you ride out here. You mustn't let it upset you too much. It hurts, of course. Harley was a mighty good man and we all thought the world of him. But . . . these things happen."

She met his glance. She was biting her lips to still their quivering and her fine eyes were wet. Abruptly she turned away and went into the ranch house.

Gib Dawson's voice went low and weary. "Been afraid of something like this. It's going to ride my conscience. Do your best for Harley, son. When you're ready, let me know. I'll read a service."

They buried Harley Jacks on the open slope where the sun hit fully. Stewart Hubbard, composed and quiet again, walked beside Gib Dawson as he came along on his creaking crutch. The old cattleman stood at the head of the grave and read the brief service from a small and ancient *Prayer Book*. Stewart stood close to Wade Stagmire and he saw her lips silently forming the words as Gib Dawson read.

" 'Man, that is born of woman . . .' "

It was soon done with and Dawson and the girl went back to the ranch house, and by the time the grave was filled and carefully mounded, Stewart Hubbard had headed back for town. Buck Hare walked stiffly into the bunkhouse, his face a hard mask, his jaw set. Noyo, his black eyes forlorn, went into the cook shack. For a space, Bill Vessels and Wade Stagmire were alone.

"All right," said Vessels harshly, "that's done. We've lost a good friend and comrade, Wade. I been watching you and you've been doing some heavy thinking. I've been trying to think myself but I ain't reached any sound answers. Mebbe you have?"

"Yeah," admitted Stagmire slowly, "I've been thinking, all right, and I've got a few ideas. Call them guesses and any guess can be wrong. Only one thing we can be reasonably sure of, and that is that it wasn't cattle this time."

"But if not cattle . . . then what?"

"It could be . . . timber. Or range. Like this, Bill. Let's suppose a few things. For instance, let's suppose that Lawrey's main reason for rustling Anchor cattle wasn't just to get cheap beef. Let's suppose that kind of business could serve two or three purposes at once. The profit Lawrey was making off that rustled beef was just gravy. But what Lawrey was really after was to weaken Gib Dawson down so far he'd finally go bust. Once Gib was broke, he'd have to let go of this valley range, and then Lawrey could move in on it. From what you and the others have said from time to time, I gather that's the way Lawrey's got hold of several parcels of range."

"Yeah, that's the way he's done more than once," agreed Vessels. "But what's this valley range got to do with some damn' whelp gunning Harley Jacks over on Hester Creek? How does that add up?"

Stagmire twisted up a cigarette. "I'm still just supposing, Bill. But this is lumber country, and,

169

while I don't know much about the lumbering business, I'd make an offhand guess that that great stand of redwood on Hester Creek is worth a mighty big chunk of money. Right now that stand of timber belongs to Gib Dawson. But if somebody managed to get hold of this range, then they'd get that timber, wouldn't they?"

A cold gleam sparked and deepened in Vessels's blue eyes. "Hah!" he exclaimed. "Now that does make sense, Wade . . . it surely does. Now mebbe somebody who had just such ideas was prowling through that Hester Creek timber when Harley Jacks bumped into them. And mebbe, to keep Harley from bringing the word to old Gib, they gunned Harley. Would that be it?"

"Something of the sort could have happened," returned Stagmire. "But remember, we're just guessing and supposing. We don't know a thing for certain. So let's keep our mouths shut until we know something definite. But we're not going to forget about Harley . . . not for a minute are we ever going to forget. Now you go on and give Buck something to lean on a little. He's taken this awful rough."

Gib Dawson was waiting for Stagmire on the ranch house porch. When Stagmire crossed over, Dawson sat silently for a little time, puffing grimly at his pipe. Finally he said: "You stepped in real handsome to help me get Stewart's thoughts away from that pencil, son . . . but I could see in your eyes that you might have some ideas about it. What are they?"

"Suppose you answer me a question, Gib," Stagmire said. "Who would be wandering around through a great stand of timber who would have need of a pencil? A new pencil, only a little used. And a pencil that hadn't laid out any longer than the time Harley was shot. Which must have been yesterday, sometime. What's your answer there, Gib?"

" 'Most anybody might pack a pencil," said Dawson cautiously. "Even a cowhand. But . . . it'd most likely be a stubbed-down one, not a new one, fresh-pointed. On the other hand, somebody who was cruising timber an' making a lot of figures and notes . . ."

"Now," drawled Stagmire softly, "you're thinking like I'm thinking."

Dawson cleared his throat. "But that Hester Crick timber is my timber, boy. And why should anybody be cruising timber that's mine? I sure didn't order it done."

"Could be," murmured Stagmire, "that whoever was having that timber cruised figured to own it someday. Ever think of that, Gib?"

Dawson scowled thoughtfully. "Go on . . . go on. You're leading up to something. Keep talking, son."

"Like this," said Stagmire. "You lose enough cows, you go bust, Gib. You go bust, you lose your range. You lose your range, you lose that Hester Creek timber. And somebody else gets it . . . who wants it. That's my answer."

The cattleman passed a gnarled hand slowly across his face. "I've thought of that," he admitted, "and I didn't want to think it. Because you know where it leads?"

"Yeah," agreed Stagmire gravely, "it leads to them who could use that timber. For instance, to Jared Hubbard. And you hate that thought and so do I. Because we're both thinking of Stewart Hubbard. And we'd both rather cut off our right arm than hurt that girl. But we just buried a good man . . . one of our own . . . and we found a pencil . . . and, damn it all, Gib, where else can the trail lead?"

Dawson's grizzled head rocked up and down slowly. "I know, boy . . . I know. I believe I told you once that Ruel Tedrow had tackled me about my Hester Crick timber . . . wanting to know what I'd take for that stand. I told him where to go. He must have been acting for Jared Hubbard. So, not being able to buy it from me, they aim to use other means. But did they have to shoot Harley Jacks, just because he caught them cruising my timber on the sly? God sakes, boy, I can't believe Jared Hubbard would stand for anything like that."

Stagmire shrugged. "That's the angle I can't figure at all," he admitted. "But there must be

172

a right answer somewhere. I'm going looking for that answer, Gib. It ain't here, in this valley. It's got to be in town. So I'm heading there. I don't know how long I'll be gone. Maybe a day or two, maybe a week. But if it takes ten years, I'm going to get at the bottom of this affair."

"You're not going in alone, boy? Why, they'll be laying for you and they'll guess what you're up to, you go prowling around. And then you'll get just what Harley got."

"They won't catch me off guard, like they must have caught Harley," declared Stagmire. "I'll be watching for anything like that. So I'm going alone. Bill and Buck will have to stay here and keep an eye on things. Still cattle to guard . . . and other things. This game is getting plenty rough, so we can't afford to let down our guard anywhere. But don't you worry about me. Knowing what I know, hunting for what I'm going to be hunting for, they won't catch me looking the wrong way."

"Mebbe," said Dawson despondently, "was I to offer to sell my Hester Crick timber to Hubbard, they'd leave me and my crew alone. And then I wouldn't have the deaths of any more good men to ride always on my shoulders."

"No," rapped Stagmire sharply. "Forget that kind of talk, Gib. It's all wrong. For one thing, that would be letting Harley down, flat. For

173

another, should you make 'em that offer, they'd figure they had you over a barrel and you'd have to take their price. They'd rob you. So we sit tight, and we run down some trails. And then we'll see."

Chapter Fourteen

Stagmire met up with the fog again, some half mile in from the mouth of the Sotoyome River. It came on the wings of a soaring ocean wind that whipped up the narrow cañon, built a solid moan in the timber tops, and filled the world with a dripping chill. Stagmire hunched his shoulders and bowed his head into the wind's wet drive as he rode.

In heading in to Castle City, Stagmire was well aware of the fact that he might very well have no luck at all in picking up any true lead on the shooting of Harley Jacks. For this country was like the fog that shrouded it—it was big and wild enough to swallow up and blot out anything. And he hadn't a thing to go on except a theory, a man's death and a yellow pencil, all of which might be or might not be related in fact.

Yet he had to make a try at unraveling the tangle, for it was certain that by sitting back at Anchor and doing nothing but wait, this thing would not solve itself. Here in town, if he looked and listened and perhaps asked enough shrewd questions, he might just possibly run across something. If he didn't, then the next move was definitely that he tackle Jared Hubbard directly again, and by hard and persistent questioning uncover some truths.

For the conviction was growing and strengthening in Stagmire all the time that the rustling of Anchor cattle, past and present, while serious enough to Gib Dawson's affairs, was but a minor card in this game. The more a man thought of it and considered all the angles, the more certain this conclusion became. Because it made hard, cold sense, and all the strings concerned tied in so neatly. Through Frank Lawrey and his operations, to Ruel Tedrow—and from Tedrow inevitably to Jared Hubbard.

With the final pot in the tricky game, that magnificent stand of redwood timber on Hester Creek. For timber was the big item in this country, not cows, or a little stretch of inland valley range. Timber was the real wealth along this wild coast and all else was a minor sideline.

But the hell of it was, mused Stagmire, it was as he had said to Gib Dawson. If Jared Hubbard was tied in with this thing, and proven so, it was going to hurt Stewart Hubbard savagely. That slim, vivid girl, with those fine, lovely eyes. With her obvious honesty and unswerving character. And the compelling charm and lure of her. A man could not see her and forget her. In the quiet, solitary hours of a man's thoughts, she always came back to him. . . .

There was a livery and freight yard at the edge

of Castle City and this was Wade Stagmire's first port of call. Here he left his horse to be stabled out of the fog and chill. And from there Stagmire sought out Sam Alexander's big general store. He produced the pencil Noyo had found, showed it to the storekeeper.

"Got any more just like this for sale?"

Sam Alexander shook his head. "Don't handle that brand at all. But I know what it is. That's a Hubbard company pencil. They order them in big lots direct from a wholesaler in San Francisco. What about it?"

"Nothing in particular," evaded Stagmire. "Just wondering. Thanks, anyway."

From the store, Stagmire headed for the one spot in town where he knew he'd likely find someone who talked his language—the Cattleman bar. Obie Chase was behind the mahogany, poring idly over a two-weeks-old San Francisco paper. He welcomed Stagmire with a nod, set out bottle and glass. Stagmire invited Obie to have one with him.

"How about that talk that was going around the last time I was in here with Bill Vessels?" asked Stagmire.

"You mean about those two rustlers you caught up with along the Sotoyome? Hell, that's all forgotten. Big talk now is all about the heavy rush orders the mill has for more lumber. They tell me that Hubbard is figuring on considerable expansion all around. More saws going in, more logging crews in the timber, more of everything. Looks like things are really going to boom. Wish I owned me a good stand of timber close in that I could sell to Hubbard. He's looking for a lot more stumpage, so the talk goes. If I had some I could sell him, I'd be able to get out from behind this damned bar for good and all and away from drunks and souses like that one yonder." Obie Chase jerked his head.

At the far end of the room there was a squat, cast-iron heating stove, just now creaking with warmth against the day's dank chill. At a poker table near the stove a man sat, sagged forward, his head resting on his spread arms on the table top. He was snoring thickly, sodden in an alcoholic stupor.

Stagmire downed his drink, backed up to the purring stove and its welcome heat. He glanced down at the drunk, seeing a man with lank, untidy, prematurely gray hair, a man in stagged pants and calked boots.

"You pour it for them, they'll sop it up and get that way, Obie," Stagmire said mildly.

"Not me," snorted Obie. "I run a saloon, but I got no use for a souse. As I see it, liquor was made for a man to enjoy within reason, not to wallow in. Me, when I figure a man has had enough, that's all he's going to get across my bar. I never let a man drink himself down in my place and I never will. That one came stumbling in here wanting some more when he already had twice as much as he could hold. He was talking and mumbling to himself and seeing things . . . snakes, mebbe. Anyhow, I turned him down flat and told him to be on his way. Instead, he wandered over to that table and sat down there. Pretty soon the heat got him and he went to sleep. Mebbe I ought to throw him out. I would if it wasn't for this damned cold fog."

Stagmire built a cigarette, smiling slightly. "In other words, Obie . . . much as you got no use for a drunk, you wouldn't want him to lay out and develop galloping pneumonia, is that it? A stranger to you, is he?"

"Not exactly," Obie answered, mechanically swabbing down the bar top. "I know who he is. Name's Lytell . . . Jack Lytell. A timber cruiser by trade and a damned good one when he's sober, so the word is. Which is seldom enough, for he just can't leave the booze alone. Man, he sure had a load when he came in here, and full of fancies. Talking to himself, staring and blinking at nothing. He'd go a little quiet, then he'd sorta cringe and start mumbling to himself again, like he was seeing something that scared the hell out of him. Sure is too bad when a man with a good mind beats it to pieces with liquor that way."

Wade Stagmire had been listening without too much interest to Obie's half-grumbling words. But now of a sudden his head came up and his eyes sharpened. He half turned and took another look at the drunk. Because of the man's position, his greasy, threadbare old Mackinaw was hunched forward in folds across the back of his neck and pulled tightly across the spread of his shoulders. The front of it was pushed up somewhat under the turn of the man's unshaven jaw and there, from a breast pocket, the eraser and upper half of a yellow pencil was barely visible. Stagmire reached out and pulled the pencil free. It was an exact mate to the one Noyo had found along Hester Creek.

For a long moment Stagmire stood utterly motionless, his eyes pinched down. Then he spoke, a curt ring in his voice. "Obie, let's have something you said, over again. This drunk, you say he's a timber cruiser by trade . . . and a good one?"

"That's right," asserted the bartender. "Why . . . what about it?"

"And that when he wandered in here, he acted like he was scared of something?" probed Stagmire. "Even though he was drunk, he was scared of something?"

"Huh," grunted Obie. "Guess you never saw a souse on the verge of the shakes. When they get that way, they're scared of lots of things. They're seeing all manner of nightmares. Pink elephants dancing on the bar, green lizards crawling on the ceiling. Hell, they see things you and me can't even imagine. So they're plenty scared of . . . hey, why should you care what that guy was seeing and trying to duck away from?"

"A timber cruiser," murmured Stagmire, half to himself. "A timber cruiser, carrying the exact kind of pencil . . ." Stagmire spoke louder. "Does this fellow Lytell work for Hubbard, Obie?"

"Off and on, I guess he does. When he's sober, maybe. But just what the devil you so interested in him for, Stagmire? What . . . ?"

"I'm going to ask a favor of you, Obie," cut in Stagmire. "I'm trying to straighten out a trail. That's what I came to town for. Maybe I've stumbled onto something here . . . maybe I haven't. But I can't afford to overlook any chance. Sober, this fellow Lytell may have some mighty important answers for me. Now I'm wondering if you got a back room . . . or some place where we could keep this fellow until he sobers up?"

"I got a place," admitted Obie. "But . . ."

"Then give me a hand," rapped Stagmire. "That's where he goes. I'll pay you well for the trouble. But this is something I've got to do. When he does sober up, if I've been chasing the wrong hunch, we'll let him go and no harm done."

"Well," said Obie reluctantly, "I guess you

know what you're doing. But damn me if I can figger why you should be so interested all of a sudden in just another souse. Let's go."

Between them they pulled Jack Lytell to his feet and half carried, half dragged him through a rear door, back along a narrow hall, to dump him down on an old bunk in a small, gloomy side room. Lytell kept right on snoring. Obie went into another room and brought a couple of old blankets to spread over the man. Obie growled his disgust again.

"With the load he's packing he won't stir before tomorrow morning. Want we should lock him in?"

"Might be a good idea," Stagmire said. "Wouldn't want him to wake up some time during the night and wander off. As I say, my hunch may be a good one, and it may not. But if it is good, then I sure don't want to lose him."

They went out and Obie locked the door. "He'll wake up with one hell of a case of the shakes," predicted the bartender. "And be ready to trade his right hand for a big jolt of whiskey."

"That," said Stagmire, "could be one of the most useful angles of all. So don't you let him have a drop unless I say so. Now I'll buy you another drink for all your trouble."

Back in the barroom, which they had to themselves, Obie faced Stagmire fully. "I don't want another drink. What I want, cowboy, is to know the real why and wherefore of this monkey business with Lytell?"

Stagmire met Obie's questioning glance. "You'll keep anything I tell you strictly to yourself, Obie?"

"If I think I ought to."

"You will, I believe," said Stagmire. "Here's the story."

When Stagmire was finished, Obie's face was flushed and his eyes gleaming with anger.

"That's hard to take," he growled. "I knew Harley Jacks well and I liked him. A damned good man. Plenty of times I've swapped talk with him across my bar. This hunch of yours, then, is that mebbe Jack Lytell was present when Harley was shot, that he's scared, and that he's drunk himself into the shakes trying to forget it . . . and can't?"

"Something like that," admitted Stagmire.

Obie Chase pinched a pursed lower lip with thumb and forefinger, scowling thoughtfully. He spoke slowly. "I can see your point, all right. But you got to remember there's lots of other timber cruisers besides Jack Lytell, and that he's a known souse. And souses get that way, so overloaded they see things and talk to themselves."

"That's right," said Stagmire. "This may be a completely empty bird's nest, Obie. But I got to start somewhere."

"That makes some sense," agreed Obie. "And

I sure hope you're on the right trail. Now we'll have that drink, only I'll buy."

Instead of a drink, Stagmire took a cigar and was just lighting up when the street door swung and the gross figure of Mitch Caraway, the town marshal, pushed through. Caraway paraded his big stomach up to the bar, eyeing Stagmire with no friendliness at all. Obie Chase, his face bland and unrevealing, waited for Caraway's order.

"Rye," said the marshal huskily.

He poured a stiff drink, downed it, and then, as he rang a coin on the bar, asked: "Seen Jack Lytell around, Chase?"

The blandness in Obie's face deepened. "Yeah. He was in here a while ago, soused to the ears. I wouldn't let him have any more, so he mumbled around for a time, then faded out."

"What was he mumblin' about?"

Obie shrugged. "Just some kind of drunk talk. I didn't pay any attention. Who ever pays any account to a drunk's muttering?"

Stagmire, paying strict attention, saw a certain relief run across Caraway's bloated features.

"I guess that's right," opined the marshal. "Well, if Lytell shows up again in here, hold him and get word to me, will you?"

"What you want him for?" asked Obie. Then he added with a dry sarcasm: "Don't tell me the law's decided to get tough with drunks in this town? If it is, then on pay nights you'll have your

184

pokey stacked six deep with soused lumberjacks and mill hands."

"Oh, no, nothin' like that," mumbled Caraway hurriedly. "Only . . . Jack Lytell is a mighty shrewd timber cruiser when he's sober, and they're needin' a cruiser up at Camp Four on Bacon Ridge, so Ruel Tedrow asked me to see could I locate Lytell for him."

Caraway gave Wade Stagmire another surly glance, then went heavily out.

Stagmire took his cigar from his lips, knocked off the ash, blew a pale line of smoke from faintly smiling lips. "Obie, I like my hunch better all the time. Did you see the relief on that fat slob's face when you told him you hadn't paid any attention to Lytell's mumblings?"

"Damned right I saw it." Obie was emphatic about this. "You know, Stagmire, I'm getting a funny feeling about this. Now I wouldn't be at all surprised that the only reason Jack Lytell will be alive tomorrow morning is because we've got him locked up safe. Somebody could be bad worried about Lytell and what Lytell knows."

"Pretty good reasoning," said Stagmire, "but it's got a hole in it. If somebody wanted to close Lytell's mouth for good, why would they wait this long?"

"To make it look good, so there'd be no kick-back. Like this, for instance. They see that Lytell gets started on a spree. They let him be seen wandering around town, all soused up. Come night he disappears. Mebbe he never shows up again. Or mebbe, later on, his body is found, washed up on some beach. To all intents and purposes, while he's blind drunk, he's blundered around in the fog and fallen off the headland into the surf. It's happened before. So Jack Lytell is buried and that's that."

Obie made an aimless pass at the bar top with the tail of his apron. "Here's something else. Caraway was lying in his teeth when he said Ruel Tedrow had need of a cruiser up at Camp Four on Bacon Ridge. I got a brother-in-law who's a teamster. He was in here yesterday evening, just passing idle talk. He'd been busy as hell for the past three weeks, hauling gear away from Camp Four, because all the good timber on Bacon Ridge has been logged, and Camp Four is being abandoned. Cowboy, sure as shooting, we're on the trail of something."

Chapter Fifteen

It would be a couple of hours before night would fully fall on Castle City. Yet in many places lights were already glowing because of the fog's wet murk. When the day shift at the mill came off work, there would be plenty of activity along the streets, but at this moment only a few humans were abroad and these, as Wade Stagmire passed them, were impersonal, shadowy figures that loomed suddenly and just as suddenly vanished again in the dripping mists.

Footsteps on the moisture-slimed boardwalks were muffled and carried but a little way; the only sounds of movement were the droning whine of the mill's saws and that distant, booming overtone that was the might of ocean waters beating against the headlands.

Stagmire, prowling the town, located other bars than the Cattleman, and into each of these he dropped, almost unobtrusively, a lean, still-faced man in spurred boots, jeans, and a sheepskin-lined canvas coat, the broad collar of which was beaded with fog moisture. He had left his belt and holster with his saddle gear in the livery stable, but his gun was tucked into the waistband of his jeans, where his jacket covered it.

Clothed in the armor of tending strictly to his

own business, Stagmire ran into neither hostility nor proffered friendship. At the bars he would buy a short drink and dawdle over it for a time, apparently concerned entirely with his own affairs. He asked no questions and seemed to pay little attention to his surroundings. Yet his ears were wide for any chance word and he missed little of what went on around him. He had little hope of running across anything specific, yet in Jack Lytell he had hopes of one broad lead, and sheer chance had given him that. Perhaps chance would reward him some other way, if he searched hard enough. So it happened that in the third bar he stopped at, he listened to some talk that backed up what Obie Chase had told him.

A pair of lumberjacks was at the bar, fresh in from the woods, a brawny pair in stagged pants and calked boots and ragged Mackinaws, the reckless hardihood of their trade showing in their weathered faces. Apparently Mitch Caraway had been in this place not long before in his search for Jack Lytell, and had given for his reason the same one he had voiced in the Cattleman.

"Caraway's lyin' like hell about somethin'," declared one of the lumberjacks bluntly. "Jack Lytell is a good cruiser, all right . . . none better. But he sure ain't wanted up at Camp Four on Bacon Ridge. Because we finished cuttin' out that piece of country a month ago. Ain't that right, Jerry?"

The other lumberjack nodded. "Camp Four and all its gear has been moved south to Salmon Creek. Caraway don't know what he's talkin' about."

The bartender laughed. "I'll take your word for it, boys. I was only tellin' you what Caraway told me. I agree with you that Mitch Caraway is anything but a ball of fire between the ears."

Stagmire went out into the fog again, his mind weighing and probing all possibilities. It seemed plain enough that Mitch Caraway was lying about his reason for wanting to locate Jack Lytell. And if this were so, wasn't it reasonable to suspect that he was lying to cover up the real reason? And if so—why?

Stagmire added up all he knew for certain. He knew that Jack Lytell was a well-known timber cruiser, respected for his ability when sober. He knew that right now Lytell lay in a drunken sleep in one of Obie Chase's back rooms and he knew that when Lytell first appeared in the Cattleman, the man had been full of drunken jitters that caused him to mumble to himself and cringe as though in fear of something. But he had to remember that this could very well be nothing more than black fantasies evolved in the disordered chaos of a mind bludgeoned and shattered by an overdose of alcohol. Again, the real reason could be far more stern and significant.

Two other things he knew for certain. He had found the exact mate to the pencil picked up on Hester Creek in Lytell's Mackinaw pocket, which also could mean much or nothing. Finally he knew that Mitch Caraway was anxiously trying to locate Jack Lytell, and flatly lying about his reason for doing so. Under orders from Ruel Tedrow. . . .

Stagmire shook his head bleakly. That was part of the trail that he did not like. From Jack Lytell to Mitch Caraway. From Caraway to Tedrow. From Tedrow—where? Maybe to Jared Hubbard, and if that were so, then there was Stewart Hubbard to be hurt. . . .

Stagmire shook his head again. There could be triumph and retribution along this trail, but there could also be tragedy that would wound deep and leave never-healing scars. His mood turned dark and grim as he headed again for the Cattleman bar. He would, he decided, spend the night there, even if he had to sleep on a table. For he was going to make very sure that no one got at a sobering-up Jack Lytell before he did.

With night's approach, the fog gloom steadily deepened. Lights that showed here and there were just round, bleary, yellow blooms, palely furtive, spreading that air of furtiveness across the whole deepening scene. Once, against one such thin glow, Stagmire glimpsed a figure silhouetted, quickly viewed and as quickly sliding from sight again. The figure of a man, lank and long-bodied. A vague touch of familiarity came to Stagmire, but remained for only a moment, what with the other things on Stagmire's mind. The brief glimpse had not provided enough to fix the matter in his busy thoughts. And besides, in this murk a man's eyes could play him tricks.

His return route to the Cattleman led Stagmire past Sam Alexander's store and there, against the generous light within, stood a figure in the doorway that was beyond possible mistaking. It was Stewart Hubbard. She had on her scarlet Mackinaw, but her head was bare, and Wade Stagmire was startled at the warm, swift gust of feeling that flooded him at the sight of her.

Since the day he had first laid eyes on Stewart Hubbard, there had been a growing consciousness in Wade Stagmire of this girl. He had tried to keep his thoughts away from her, for there was a strong streak of realism in Stagmire. Stewart Hubbard was the niece of a very rich and powerful man. Someday, no doubt, she would be sole owner of a big and wealthy lumber concern. While Wade Stagmire was an ordinary saddle hand, a man with a murder charge hanging over him. And these were cold facts that no sensible, balanced, fair-minded man could ignore.

Yet, no matter what his thoughts and feelings of the past were, they were completely wiped out by the emotion that flooded him now. It was

191

a rush of feeling that was tremendous, knocking all else out of his head but that overwhelming consciousness of her as she stood there, at this blinding moment. In this one glimpse she had suddenly become the center of his entire universe. Never had he been so profoundly shaken. He climbed the store's low steps and stood before her, hat in hand.

She held a market basket, loaded with groceries, and Stagmire seized desperately at this excuse. "I don't know how far you've got to lug that basket, Miss Hubbard . . . but I'd sure admire to pack it for you."

It could have been the intensity of his glance, or something in the timbre of his voice that got some hint of his feelings across to her. At any rate she went very still, her lovely eyes meeting his. Then an almost girlish shyness touched her and her glance fell. Her voice was low and sweet.

"You . . . startled me. But if you'd like to help . . . that would be nice of you. Usually Uncle Jared's housekeeper, Missus Strang, does the kitchen shopping, but she was very busy this afternoon, so I offered to do it for her. . . ."

She had handed over the basket as she spoke and now she tucked a slim hand under Stagmire's arm and swung down the steps beside him. She was as near to him as the touch of her hand and her presence rocked his senses. They went along in silence for some little distance before he could think of anything to say, and then his remark was quite commonplace.

"This fog sure tangles me up. Gives me the feeling that at any second I might step off into nothing and end up nowhere."

She laughed softly. "I know what you mean. It takes the set order and solidity out of the world and makes everything ghostly and unreal."

"That's how it seemed to me when I saw you just now at the door of the store," he said carefully. "I couldn't believe that you were real. Then I knew you were . . . so very real. The most completely real person I've ever known in all my life."

He felt her draw a little away from him, although her hand still rested in the crook of his arm. She laughed again, lightly, but it was a laugh not entirely free of a slight unsteadiness. "This fog, Mister Stagmire, certainly does addle you."

"Not mister any more," he suggested swiftly.

She was silent for a step or two and then, in that soft way: "Very well, Wade. What brings you to town? That . . . that terrible thing about . . . Harley Jacks?"

"Yes. I'm looking for a trail."

She shivered, drew closer to him again. "I've been trying to put it out of my mind, but without much success. I keep remembering the look on Buck Hare's face when . . . when we buried

Harley. And the sadness in Mister Gib's eyes. . . ."

"It takes time to blunt things of that sort," Stagmire told her gravely. "The months and the years can mellow to some extent the deep hurts of life. But those hurts can leave other obligations besides mere memories."

Her hand tightened on his arm. "Now . . . now you scare me. There's the will for vengeance in you, isn't there?"

"Being human, I couldn't be otherwise. Somebody has to be taught a lesson, and perhaps a mighty grim one. For if they're not, then next time it could be Bill Vessels, or Buck Hare . . . or maybe Gib Dawson."

"Or . . . or you?"

"Possibly. But I don't think of that. Or worry about it, either. A man has to be a fatalist about such things, Stewart."

She showed a little burst of fierceness that startled him. "Why can't they leave Mister Gib alone? He's such a dear old man. There is a great sweetness in him. He'd never harm a soul in this world if they'd only leave him alone."

"They? Who are . . . they, Stewart?"

She did not answer for a moment. Then: "That scares me too, Wade. I'm afraid of where this trail you're seeking could lead."

Stagmire knew exactly what she was referring to. "Never be afraid of anything that isn't real, girl. And nothing is real about this . . . yet. And no matter what might come from it, you certainly need never feel any responsibility."

"If it is the fault of any Hubbard in any way," she said with quiet emphasis, "then I must share that fault. Wade . . . do, do you think Uncle Jared . . . ?"

"No," cut in Stagmire quickly. "No matter how the evidence may point, for some reason I just can't swallow such a possibility. It's a feeling I have that such a possibility just doesn't add up. I really mean that, Stewart."

Again he felt the quick pressure of her hand, and her words were very soft. "Thank you, Wade Stagmire."

They were getting along toward the southern edge of town. Off to their right the rasping snarl of the mill's saws, as they bit into the heart of another redwood log, tore through the fog with a measured, harsh insistence. But aside from that, here for this moment, these two people were completely alone. Stagmire slowed his step, looking down at her.

"I'd like to tell you again how lovely you are, Stewart."

There was no shyness in the glance she put on him now, just a great and sober questing, a complete honesty, searching for its like. And she seemed to find it, for her lips parted breathlessly, and her slender throat pulsed with forming words.

And then, before she could utter those words,

the challenge came out of the fog behind them, harsh and droningly savage, brittle and wicked as a whip crack.

"Stagmire!"

He went away from her like some startled, desperate animal, away in a swinging, whirling leap. The basket of groceries dropped to the ground, scattered wildly. Stagmire plunged farther to the side, but two things on his mind. First, to get far enough away from Stewart so she'd be well out of the line of fire. Second, to get at his gun. He knew what to expect. At a time like this a man's mind either locked up solidly and refused to function at all, or it opened to thoughts that traveled like lightning flashes. Stagmire's mind wasn't locked.

He was remembering now that furtive figure he'd seen in the dim glow of a light, just before he'd come to Sam Alexander's store and seen Stewart standing in the store doorway. A figure half seen and half guessed at, like some figment of the fog, yet which had left with him for a short moment a vague sense of familiarity. Now it was the tone of the voice that threw this challenge that wiped out all vagueness and made recognition real. It was a voice he had heard before, on that day in the Cattleman bar, when he'd first met Bill Vessels. The hard and wicked drone of Price Mabry. Price Mabry—gunfighter.

Gun flame winked, thin and lashing in the

drifting, darkening murk—flame that made little round blobs of light, which opened and closed—opened and closed, while the pound of the gun was a heavy, coughing thud. Stagmire kept going wide, low-crouched now, the butt of his gun hard in his palm, the weapon dragging clear.

He heard Mabry cursing venomously because he'd missed, and he couldn't understand just how or why the man had missed. At another time and place another man had come at him, just like this—a man named Dodd Evans—come at him from in back and unexpectedly. And that man had missed him, too. It was something he just couldn't understand. How far could a man's luck be stretched—how far?

He threw his first answering shot, threw it at another wink of gun flame that stabbed in the fog. Then he ran straight in on that spot, shooting as he went. Two—three—four times, shooting until the hammer of his gun clicked uselessly on a cartridge already exploded.

He ran right into a reeling figure. He slashed savagely at the head of the figure with his empty gun, but missed the blow, for the figure was already falling, crumpling away from him. Stagmire tripped, fell to his hands and knees. He came up and around, lunging back. But there was nothing in front of him now, nothing but fog and steadily deepening gloom. Yet, at his feet there was something. A lank figure, sprawled and still.

197

A voice was calling to him, Stewart Hubbard's voice, with a sobbing dread in it: "Wade . . . Wade!"

He stumbled a little as he went to meet her, panting like a man who had just gone through some tremendous physical effort. Then she was in his arms, close to him, clinging to him, and she was wailing like a hurt child.

"Wade . . . you're not hit . . . you're all right . . . all right . . . Wade . . . ?"

"Yeah," he gulped hoarsely. "All right."

It was like stepping right from the raw pit of hell into some great paradise. He buried his face in her fog-jeweled hair, which smelled of all the fine, clean reaches of the sea. Here was the peak moment of his life, vaguely dreamed of only a few minutes ago, and now reality. Terror had come and gone and here was Stewart— in his arms. He murmured her name, over and over. . . .

But soon there were voices, shouting, and the thud of the running feet of men. They came blundering through the murk, profane with excitement, stirred and avid from the rumbling pound of guns. Stagmire set Stewart a little apart from him.

"Quick. You've got to get out of here. There'll be questions, maybe more rough play. Hurry!"

She brushed aside his warding arm. "No! I'm staying right here with you."

Before he could make her understand, the first of the blundering crowd reached them, milling around like curious animals. In the vanguard was the gross bulk of Mitch Caraway, town marshal.

"What's goin' on here? What's all the shootin' about?"

"Hell, Mitch!" cried a lumberjack. "You blind? There's a man down, right at your feet."

"Yeah," said Wade Stagmire bleakly, "there is. It's Price Mabry. And he asked for it."

Now he was cool and quiet again and he faced them watchfully. Mitch Caraway dropped heavily to one knee, pawing at the inert figure of Price Mabry. He swore explosively, lurched to his feet.

"He's dead," Caraway blurted. "You killed him. Mister, I warned you . . . !"

"What is it, Mitch?" The words were curt, arrogant with authority. This was Ruel Tedrow who now came shouldering his way through the crowd, and at his heels was Frank Lawrey.

"Price Mabry, Mister Tedrow," said Caraway. "This fellow here killed him. He admits it. He shot Mabry to rags."

"Price Mabry!" exclaimed Frank Lawrey. "Not another good man of mine? That's three this fellow Stagmire has done for. I say the man's gun crazy. I say something should be done about him . . . and quick!"

Ruel Tedrow stepped up to within a stride of

Stagmire. Tedrow rolled forward on his toes, his heavy shoulders bulled and slightly hunched, his fists knotted and swinging restlessly, a man aching to throw a blow.

Wade Stagmire still held to his empty gun. Now he balanced it easily in his hand. "You try anything, Tedrow, and I'll sure part your hair with this gun. I tell you, Mabry asked for it. He came up in back of me and was shooting before I ever laid a hand on my gun. So, don't try and push your luck . . . or you won't have any."

The crowd had thickened steadily and those lately arrived, pushing and shoving to get close enough to see what it was all about, made the circle of onlookers weave and sway. In the mêlée, no one seemed to notice Stewart Hubbard, no one that is except a dapper figure in overcoat and muffler who the crowd opened to let through. It was Jared Hubbard. His voice was not loud, but it carried the ring of authority that brought an uneasy quiet.

"Stewart! What are you doing here, girl? I thought I heard shots. This is no place for you."

She darted over to him. "Uncle Jared. Oh, I'm glad you're here. Make these fools leave Wade alone. They don't understand. They . . ."

"Quiet!" rapped Hubbard sternly. "I don't understand this and I want to know. Tedrow, what happened?"

"A shooting scrape, Mister Hubbard," answered

Tedrow smoothly. "That Anchor rider, Stagmire, just killed another of Frank Lawrey's riders . . . Price Mabry. Apparently shot him down in cold blood. And . . ."

"That's not true!" flamed Stewart Hubbard. She pulled away from her uncle, ran over to Stagmire's side, where she faced Ruel Tedrow hotly. "It was exactly as Wade says. That . . . that other man shot at Wade first. He was close behind us!"

"Lady," broke in Frank Lawrey glibly, "that can't be the straight of it. If Price Mabry had shot first from close in, he wouldn't have missed. I say again that this fellow Stagmire is gun crazy and too dangerous to be let run loose. I say . . ."

"Wait a minute!" It was Jared Hubbard again, and now his tone had plenty of bite to it. "I don't understand all of this, but of one thing I'm very sure. If my niece witnessed this affair and she says that Mabry shot first, then that is how it was. No man can question her word. She doesn't lie. But, Stewart, I want to know about you. I want to know how it was you were here, with this fellow Stagmire. How . . . ?"

"Suppose I explain everything right from the first, Mister Hubbard," cut in Stagmire. "This is what happened . . . and how . . . all of it."

The crowd quieted to listen. Jared Hubbard gave Stagmire a swift searching glance, nodded curtly. "Very well."

"I happened to come by Sam Alexander's store," Stagmire explained. "I saw Miss Hubbard just leaving there. She'd been marketing and had a heavy basket of groceries on her arm. I offered to carry them home for her. We were walking along here when Mabry came up behind us. He yelled my name, once, then started to shoot. I got away from Miss Hubbard as fast as I could so she'd be in the clear. While I was doing that, Mabry had a couple of tries at me before I was able to shoot back. Don't ask me how he missed. I wouldn't know. But he did. And I had better luck. Now that's the straight of it."

"And the exact truth," seconded Stewart staunchly. "Every last word of it."

She had hold of Stagmire's arm again and she faced her uncle and Tedrow and all the crowd proudly and defiantly. But she was drawing on her courage and Wade Stagmire knew it, for he could sense her trembling.

A listening lumberjack spoke gruffly. "Whatever Miss Stewart says is the straight of it, that goes across with me. And, Lawrey, any talk you try and make that Price Mabry was just a poor, inoffensive saddle pounder is a lot of guff, and you know it. He was anything but that. He was a mean and surly devil, always with a chip on his shoulder and with his gun free and ready. My vote is that he just asked for somethin' . . . and got it."

Mitch Caraway swung heavily toward the speaker. "I'll decide on that, Jenkins. You keep your . . ."

"Wrong, Caraway," said Jared Hubbard crisply, "I'll decide. I say once more . . . my niece's word is good. There's no point in pushing this thing further." He turned to Stagmire. "Do you know of any good reason why this fellow Mabry should have come at you this way?"

Stagmire shrugged. "There was a minor affair in the Cattleman bar some time back, when Mabry made a few threats. And then there was that affair when a couple of his own stripe didn't come off so well in an attempted raid on Gib Dawson's cattle. Maybe Mabry was remembering that and had an idea about evening up. But I wouldn't bet on it. For from what I saw of Mabry, he struck me as being a pretty cold-blooded proposition and looking out for himself at all times."

For a long moment Jared Hubbard studied Stagmire keenly. Then he nodded. He turned to the girl. "We'll go along home now, Stewart." And to Tedrow he said: "There's plenty of work ahead of us, Ruel. I want to see you at the office within an hour."

Stewart still clung to Stagmire's arm. He bent his head and spoke softly to her. "Go along with your uncle. Everything will be all right now. And . . . for my money, you're one complete little thoroughbred."

She gave him a long, still look, biting a little at lips that quivered slightly. The reaction to this savage affair had her fully. Wordlessly she obeyed Stagmire. She stepped close to her uncle, and they went away into the dusk.

Wade Stagmire watched them disappear, then whirled on Mitch Caraway, his voice running low and cold. "This for you, you blustering chunk of rancid blubber. You try pushing me around any more and I'll take that damned badge off you and choke you with it. Get out of my way."

He walked straight in on Caraway and Caraway got out of the way. The crowd beyond opened up to let Stagmire through. And after he had gone, the lumberjack, Jenkins, said: "Price Mabry just thought he was tough. That fellow yonder really is."

Chapter Sixteen

The Hubbard home was roomy and comfortable, staunchly built of the lumber that had made the Hubbard empire—redwood. It was well, if not luxuriously, furnished. There was a cheery crackling in the big stone fireplace of the living room. Jared Hubbard, doffing his hat and muffler and overcoat, backed up to the flames, hands spread, and looked at his niece gravely. When he spoke, his tone was surprisingly gentle.

"Tell me about it, my dear. You came to know this fellow, Stagmire, I presume, through your visits out at Gib Dawson's ranch. I am surprised, of course, that your interests should turn that way. For after all, the man is only a cowhand and a strange one at that, of whom we know very little. There seems to be a streak of violence in him, also. He just killed a man. Justifiably, perhaps, but hardly a pleasant fact to consider. And from all I hear, Mabry was not the first."

Here in the warm, protective seclusion of her own home, the evening's savage interlude seemed to have moved far away. Stewart had begun to steady down, though there was a strange tumult beating in her heart that did not have its cause in gun flame and the grisly outcome of man's capacity for black, raw hate. She answered her uncle gravely.

"No matter, Uncle Jared. I'm sure that whatever Wade Stagmire has done, his actions were justified, just as they were today. And Uncle Jared, there are some things in this world that simply cannot be reduced to the cold science of bloodless figures and calculations. There are things that make for human happiness that cannot be precisely blueprinted or reduced to a formula. Wade Stagmire is a good man. In my heart I am very sure of that."

As she spoke these last words, a warm and deepening glow shone in her wide, lovely eyes. Hubbard, watching, did not miss this. "You have become very fond of Wade Stagmire, haven't you, Stewart?"

He watched intently as she considered this, and he saw her eyes widen, saw that warm light deepen and deepen in them, saw her whole face sweeten, saw her go slightly breathless. She nodded, with a slow, definite certainty.

"Yes, Uncle Jared, I have. I know now why a certain strangeness came over me the moment I first saw him. I know now why I've kept remembering him, why I've thought of him so much and so often. And then, out there, when that Mabry person yelled at him like some slinking animal about to spring, when the shooting started and I knew what deadly danger Wade Stagmire was in, I suddenly knew . . . why I had felt about Wade as I did."

"Child, you love that man."

Hubbard saw her go a long way away from him, retiring into the secluded sanctity of her own thoughts, while she honestly considered this. And then she came back, her eyes very steady, while she nodded.

"Yes, Uncle Jared . . . I do."

Jared Hubbard had spent a lifetime devoted to the amassing of possessions, of wealth and all the concrete things that money could buy. A widower early in life, it had never occurred to him to marry again; he had been too busy building this lumber empire of his. Yet, of later years there had been times when he'd begun to wonder, when a nagging voice had whispered to him that perhaps he'd missed out on a lot of life and that he'd spent too much time following the lure of false gods after all.

Just the same, it was hard to shed completely the thinking habits of a lifetime. He spent a moment lighting a cigar.

"What has this fellow Stagmire to offer you, Stewart? A cowhand and a cowhand's wages. What beyond that?"

"The love of a good man, Uncle Jared. And any woman who demands more, deserves nothing. And though it has been said many times before, it is still true . . . money can't buy happiness."

Jared Hubbard frowned through the smoke of his cigar, strangely uncomfortable because of the manner in which a lot of previously accepted props were falling away under him, and, stranger still, that he actually felt the better and more human because of this. He spoke dryly.

"But it can mightily smooth the way. Money, I mean. You are, my dear, either a very wise girl, or a very foolish one. Right now I admit I am not bold enough to say which. But I must admit one thing to which everyone has a right. And that right is to live their own life according to their own conceptions of value, and in their own way."

Swiftly she moved close to him. "Then you are not going to object, Uncle Jared?"

He looked down into the misty, brimming sweetness in her eyes. "Child," he said, "with some surprise I find I am not the cold-blooded, calculating, money-making machine that I once thought I was. I find myself rather eagerly considering a brand-new set of values. And while I'm not very good at expressing myself where sentiment is concerned, I am really tremendously fond of you, and right now I know that your future happiness means more to me by far than anything else in this world. So . . . if Wade Stagmire is the man who can bring you such happiness, then I am content."

Immediately a swarming tempest of affection was upon him, his cigar was knocked from his hand, arms were about his neck, and the moistness of tears and eager lips were on his cheek. Then Stewart burrowed her head into his shoulder and wept a little.

"I was so afraid . . . so horribly afraid, Uncle Jared. I . . . I still am . . . thinking what might have happened. . . ."

Jared Hubbard tightened an arm about her and he said a surprising thing. "I had a good look into his eyes out there. And I agree with you, my dear. Wade Stagmire is a good man. There is a violence in him, but I think it is the kind of violence that is good for a man to own to. The kind of violence that will enable him carefully to guard and protect all that he may possess. Now then, you'll have to bring that fellow around, so that I may come to know him better."

Chapter Seventeen

In the office of Frank Lawrey's meat cooling plant, Ruel Tedrow paced up and down, his florid face congested, his eyes baleful, his lips twisted and ugly with the bursting fury that consumed him. Slouched far down in the chair at the desk, Frank Lawrey chewed nervously at an unlighted cheroot, no hint of the false half smile on his face. Mitch Caraway stood by the door, sweating it out, watching Ruel Tedrow cautiously and fearfully with his pouched, protuberant eyes.

It was Frank Lawrey who finally spoke. "I can't figure it. Mabry had first try, he was close, and he missed. I can't figure it. . . ."

Ruel Tedrow whirled, his voice hoarse and rough. "But he did miss . . . the damned, blundering fool. Good God! Can't a man get any job done right unless he does it himself . . . ?"

Tedrow's pacing had brought him up in front of Mitch Caraway. Now he squared around to face the cringing marshal. Rolled up on his toes, his fists clenched and knotted, Tedrow seemed about to take out his spleen in a physical way on Caraway.

"And you!" spat Tedrow. "For years I've pulled strings to keep you in a fat, soft job. And now, when I want something of you, you can't deliver.

Where's Jack Lytell? Why haven't you found him?"

Mitch Caraway licked loose lips. "I've tried, Ruel . . . I'm still tryin'. I've combed this damn' town from top to bottom. I've hit up every liquor joint in the place. Everywhere it's the same story. Lytell had been there, but he ain't there now. Everywhere they say he was rubber-legged drunk. I figure he's crawled off somewhere to sleep it off. Come tomorrow he'll show up again, lookin' for some hair of the dog that bit him. I'll sure collar him then. Why are you in such a sweat to find him, anyhow?"

"None of your damned business!" raged Tedrow. "Your job is to find him, not ask me questions."

"You should have given me a better excuse," mumbled Caraway sulkily. "That talk about you wantin' him up at Camp Four on Bacon Ridge got me laughed at in a couple of places. Seems common talk that Bacon Ridge has been logged out and that Camp Four has been dismantled. I don't like bein' laughed at."

"Oh, you don't, eh?" rapped Tedrow. "Well, I'm laughing at you. Ha-ha-ha! You're nothing but a rum-soaked, blustering joke. Now get out of here and find Jack Lytell! I don't want him found tomorrow . . . I want him found tonight. Git!"

Caraway went out, heavy, lurching. Tedrow slammed the door shut behind him.

Frank Lawrey spoke past his chewed-up cheroot. "That wasn't smart, Ruel. No point in putting the spurs to Mitch that way. I admit he ain't the smartest man in the world, but he's been faithful and he's doin' his best. No, that wasn't smart."

Tedrow stamped up to the desk. "You, too? Another wise guy trying to tell me my business?"

Frank Lawrey straightened in his chair, his little eyes going cold. "Cut it fine, Ruel, cut it fine," he said thinly. "Don't try and go heavy-footed with me. It won't work. A lot of ideas that have gone sour on us are your ideas. So don't try and shift the blame. And get one thing straight. You may have a lot of people scared of you, but I'm not one of them. So . . . cut it fine."

For a moment Tedrow glared, then his glance shifted. He swung away and resumed his restless pacing. "Sorry, Frank. Only, where the hell's all our luck gone to? Sure a lot of the ideas were mine, and I still say they're good ideas. The mistake has been in trying to figure out what a man can do or can't do. Like Price Mabry. He must have had that fellow Stagmire dead to rights, and then blundered the job."

"That's right," agreed Lawrey, easing back in his chair again. "Well, all I can say is that Mabry paid a damn' big penalty for his blunder. And it leaves us 'way out on a limb as far as getting Stagmire out of circulation is concerned. Me, I was hoping we could talk the thing up enough to turn the crowd on Stagmire. Then Jared Hubbard had to step in. How do you figure that?"

"How can I figure it? In some ways you know exactly what Hubbard will say or do under a given condition. In other ways he can be damned unpredictable. He's been getting more so of late. It all seems to date from when that fellow, Stagmire, came into the picture. Stagmire! The man's blind with luck. Imagine Price Mabry having first bite, close up and from behind . . . and missing?"

"Call that part of it luck," admitted Frank Lawrey. "But let's be smart enough to admit that Stagmire's got more than luck, Ruel. The man's smart and able . . . able as hell. And not afraid of the devil. That's the real mistake we made. We didn't figure out Stagmire for what he's really worth. Jenkins was right. He's tough."

Ruel Tedrow's hands worked hungrily, the brutal twist in his face deepening. "Come the right time and place, I'll see how tough Stagmire is," he gritted. "Yeah, I'll see just how tough."

Lawrey made no answer to this. There wasn't any answer to make. Carefully laid plans had blown up. Frank Lawrey chewed on his cheroot and tried to think of new plans.

Chapter Eighteen

Wade Stagmire returned directly to the Cattleman bar from the scene of the shoot-out with Price Mabry. Even so, the word had already gone ahead of him. Obie Chase, the moment Stagmire came in, set out a stiff three fingers of whiskey. Stagmire shook his head.

"Don't want it, Obie."

"Wanting has nothing to do with it," growled Obie. "It's what you need that counts. And you need that drink. Right now you're down in the bottom of a deep, black well and you need something to jolt you out of it. This will do it. Drink it."

Stagmire hesitated, shrugged, and obeyed.

Obie said: "Now go get yourself a meal. You think you don't want that, either . . . but you do. Nothing beats the ordinary process of living to snap a man back to reality. I'll see you later."

So Stagmire went out into the fog-filled night again, located an eating house, and found that again Obie was right. He was hungry. As he ate the worst of the shadow lifted from his mind and his thoughts began to settle and grow more orderly.

From the eating place he went down to the livery barn and from the gun belt he'd left there with his saddle gear, he got another cylinder full of fresh cartridges for his gun. He dropped another half dozen loads in the pocket of his coat. He did this with a certain bleak distaste, for he certainly wasn't one to find any satisfaction in a gun's potent wickedness. But this was a grim errand he was on, and what Price Mabry had tried, another man might also attempt.

Returned to the Cattleman and settled in a chair in a far corner, Stagmire mused on this Mabry deal. He couldn't get away from the incident and he kept turning it over and over in his mind. But he did this with a growing objectivity that kept things in reasonably healthy proportion.

It was entirely possible, of course, that Mabry's sole reason for making his try was due to a gunman's perverted sense of pride. Right in this very room, on a day past, Stagmire had made Mabry take water, the day when Rocky Gentry and Burt Krug had tried to drum up courage enough to tackle Bill Vessels. And it could have been that Mabry had brooded over this until nothing would satisfy him but to try and wipe out the slight with gunsmoke.

Again, because Stagmire had downed Gentry and another Wagon Wheel rider, one Mogy Vidal, during that attempted raid on Anchor cattle, Mabry may have felt that he owed a debt of vengeance. Yet, reasonable as either of these two conclusions might be, the more Stagmire examined and considered them, the less convinced he become that either or both were the true reasons for Mabry breaking loose. He just couldn't get away from the feeling that there was a lot more behind Mabry's move.

There was, for instance, the strong possibility that Frank Lawrey had turned Mabry onto him, for Mabry was Lawrey's man and Lawrey would be remembering the day when Stagmire and Vessels had called him and laid the cards on the table. Perhaps, concluded Stagmire, looking at that meeting from this distance, it hadn't been too smart a move, after all.

The Cattleman did a rushing business that night. Castle City was a rough-and-ready town that had seen its share of wild violence. But this had been more of physical violence, fights between lumberjacks, working off an excess of animal energy they had stored up during long weeks in the woods and that a few drinks of whiskey released when the lumbering crews happened to hit town. These brawls were rugged enough, but were rarely fatal.

A shooting was something different. That was final. A man had died before a roaring, unerring gun. The word of it had gone all over town, as had the word that the man who had done Price Mabry's business for him was in the Cattleman. So men drifted in with a false casualness and furtively surveyed Wade Stagmire while they ordered and drank.

Stagmire saw this and understood the reason for it and was highly uncomfortable because of it. He felt that he was being viewed as ordinary men would look at some strange and dangerous animal. But he showed no outward sign of his distaste. He just sat quietly behind a cloud of cigar smoke and thought of Price Mabry and the savage moments surrounding Mabry's death.

One by one he discarded these thoughts until all that remained was the magic one of Stewart Hubbard and the wonder he had known when she had come into his arms and clung to him and sobbed her wild relief over his safety.

Not so very long ago had this marvel taken place, yet now it seemed almost unreal. As the magic of it came back to him, the hard, bleak lines of his face softened and Obie Chase, observing, wondered at the change. It made Stagmire look years younger, thought Obie, made him look almost boyish.

It was midnight before the last customer left. Outside, the ocean wind was a solid force, buffeting through the streets, and fog moisture dripped like rain from the eaves of buildings. Obie Chase, about to lock up, stood for a moment in the open door, sniffing the wet chill, then backed away with a shiver. At that moment it was Mitch Caraway's ponderous bulk that loomed out of the misty blackness and came pushing in. Obie eyed him with no friendliness.

"Why ain't you in bed, Mitch? I'm just about to close up. It's been a long day and I'm dead on my feet."

"Makin' a last round tryin' to locate Jack Lytell," growled the marshal. "He ain't here?"

"Do you see him?" demanded Obie with tart sarcasm. "Seems to me that a two-bit, boozy timber cruiser has become awful important all of a sudden. Why are you in such a sweat to find him?"

"Told you once. Ruel Tedrow wants him."

"Anybody'd think that Lytell was the only cruiser all up and down the redwood coast," jibed Obie. "He must owe Tedrow a dollar."

Caraway's eyes turned sulky. "Don't know anything about that. All I know is it's damn' queer how Lytell dropped out of sight all of a sudden. Plenty of people saw him around town earlier today. Now nobody knows where he is."

"Me," said Obie dryly, "I'd say that Jack Lytell was hardly important enough for folks to worry their heads keeping track of him. He's probably sleeping it off somewhere, dead to the world."

This being Caraway's own opinion, he did not argue with Obie's statement. His pouchy eyes, taking in all the room, settled for a moment on Wade Stagmire, who met the look, got to his feet, and moved up to the door.

"Just who the devil's been giving you orders to tromp on my toes, Caraway?" he demanded curtly. "Right from the first you've been trying to. Any excuse, or no excuse at all has been good enough for you to try and throw your weight at me. At whose orders, Caraway?"

Mitch Caraway tramped up and down like an uncertain elephant and his glance swung away. "All I'm interested in," he mumbled, "is findin' Jack Lytell." He backed away into the fog and the moaning wind.

Obie Chase closed the door and locked it, turned and grinned mirthlessly at Stagmire. "Mitch gets more thick-headed every day. Cowboy, more and more I'm beginning to believe that when you stashed Jack Lytell away, you got yourself a jackpot."

Stagmire nodded slowly. "That could be, Obie. I hope we can get him to talk."

"If he knows anything, he'll talk," vowed Obie. "If we have to burn it out of him. Where do you aim to sleep?"

"In a chair alongside of that stove."

Obie shook his head. "No you don't. I got room for you out back. Come on."

Obie put out the saloon lights and led the way back to his living quarters at the rear of the building where there was a spare bunk for Stagmire. In his little kitchen, Obie brewed a pot of coffee and over a scalding cup of this relaxed and rested for a moment. He spoke slowly.

"Ever since you told me about Harley Jacks, I've been thinking, Wade. Who killed him, and why? If Lytell, a timber cruiser was there, then the deal sounds like lumber business, not cattle. And in that case, if you run the trail to a finish, I wonder where it will lead. Clear to Jared Hubbard, do you think?"

Stagmire, nursing his steaming cup in both hands, shook his head slowly. "Somehow I just can't believe it of Hubbard, Obie. There's a lot I don't know about Hubbard, but from what I've seen of the man he just doesn't strike me that way."

"I'm glad to hear you say that," declared Obie. "I ain't what you'd call a bosom friend of Jared Hubbard's, but I've always admired the man, kinda. He'd done a big job here, Wade. This town was just a couple of Indian huts when Jared Hubbard moved in and began operations. In a way you might say he built this town. He started from scratch and he's grown big, damned big. And while he climbed the ladder, he took a lot of other folks up it with him, me included. I've made a pretty comfortable living here. Me, along with plenty of others, we owe a lot to Jared Hubbard."

Obie paused, sipped cautiously. "I know he can be plenty hard-boiled when he wants to, but I never did hear of a single instance when he was mean or petty or small. I know plenty of times when he's been damned liberal with families of loggers or mill men who got smashed up in their work. All in all, from where I stand, Jared Hubbard shapes up as a pretty damned fine man."

They finished their coffee and turned in. In a gray, dank dawn they were up and breakfasted. Then they went to have a look at Jack Lytell. The timber cruiser was awake but in the dregs of a partial stupor. They hauled him to his feet and steered him into Obie's kitchen. Obie shoved a cup of black coffee at him and Lytell gulped it avidly. Now the full effects of his hangover took hold of him and he began to shake. When Obie poured him another cup of coffee, Lytell shoved it aside.

"No more of that," he blurted thickly. "I need a drink of whiskey . . . a big one."

"I could furnish that, too," assured Obie, "and you'll get it, Lytell, if you open up and talk over a few things with my friend and me. When you came into my bar yesterday, what was it you were so scared of? What was it that had you cringing like a whipped dog and talking to yourself?"

Lytell hesitated, ever so slightly, then shrugged. "I don't even remember comin' into your bar. How's for that drink of whiskey?"

"No rush, no rush," said Obie smoothly. "So you can't remember coming into my bar, eh? I'll refresh your memory. You came in, looking for more hooch. You were seeing things you were afraid of and you were talking to yourself, twenty to the dozen. And you don't remember what about, or why? You plumb sure of that, Lytell?"

"I said so, didn't I?" mumbled Lytell. Then, with a sudden, raw-nerved insistence, his voice went shrill. "Damn it, where's that whiskey?"

"Gallons of it, Lytell," said Obie. "Close at hand, too. But none for you until you start remembering a little better. Tell me this. You ever been over on Hester Creek?"

Wade Stagmire, silent but intently watchful, saw sudden pallor whip through Lytell's liquor-ravished features. Here, Stagmire thought, was a man who had once been rather fine-looking— and intelligent. But his weakness for alcohol had broken up the better lines of his face, leaving them loose and furrowed, coarsening them and salting his ragged hair with too early gray. Now Lytell gulped thickly and rubbed the back of a hand across his sagging lips.

"I tell you I don't remember anything. Not even coming into your bar, Chase. All I know is I need a drink. I got to have one. I'm getting out of here. . . ."

He started to get to his feet. Stagmire reached out and pushed him back. "Not so fast, Lytell. Not so fast! We're not near through with you. Obie just asked you a question. Now I'm asking the same one. Have you ever been over on Hester Creek?"

Lytell's bleared and bloodshot eyes flickered a brief glance at Stagmire, then fell away. "I've been all over this country at one time or another. Timber cruising is my trade, and it's a trade that takes a man lots of places."

"Did it take you over on Hester Creek not so very long ago?" probed Stagmire. "Mighty wonderful stand of redwoods over there, Lytell. Gib Dawson's timber."

Lytell scrubbed his lips again with a shaking hand. His voice went shrill again. "Damn Hester Creek! What's that got to do with me needing a drink?"

Then Stagmire threw it all into one harsh, explosive question. "Why did you shoot Harley Jacks, Lytell? You killed him, didn't you, when he caught you prowling through Gib Dawson's timber along Hester Creek? Why did you do it, Lytell?"

Lytell started up, convulsed with weak anger and strong fear. "Hell with you!" he cried. "I don't know what you're talking about. You got no right to treat me this way. I'm getting out of here!"

This time Stagmire slammed him back into his chair with no show of gentleness. "You're not getting out of here, Lytell, and you get no whiskey until you talk, and talk plenty. You know

224

something I want to know. Come across with it."

From a corner shelf, Obie Chase lifted down a bottle of whiskey and a glass. He poured a small drink, downed it, and licked his lips with an emphasized appreciation. The raw, sweetish odor of the liquor drifted across the warm kitchen air. Under Stagmire's restraining hand, Jack Lytell began to shake more violently. Obie Chase spoke quietly.

"A big shot of this for you, Jack . . . after you tell Stagmire what you know."

Obie poured the glass nearly full and set it on the table just out of Lytell's reach.

Wade Stagmire tried again, his tone milder. "Now I really don't believe you killed Harley Jacks, Lytell. But of one thing I'm damned sure. You know who did. You tell us about it and you've got nothing to fear. Nobody will do anything to you. It's the other fellow we want. Who killed Harley Jacks? Was it Price Mabry?"

Jack Lytell hunched lower in his chair. His eyes were fixed on that glass of whiskey like a man hypnotized. He moaned thinly. "If . . . if I tell, he'll kill me, too. He swore he would . . . !"

Past Lytell's head, Stagmire met Obie Chase's glance. Obie nodded gravely. "That was a good hunch you had, cowboy."

Stagmire looked at Lytell again. "No he won't, Lytell. Nobody will touch you. We won't let him.

Price Mabry is dead. You've got nothing to fear from him."

"What's Mabry got to do with it?" mumbled Lytell. "I don't know anything about Price Mabry and don't give a damn. Chase, you're a damned devil. Give me that whiskey!"

He lunged for the glass, missed his grab, upset the glass. The whiskey ran across the table, dripped on the floor.

Now the room reeked with the odor of it. Jack Lytell's shaking became a series of deep shudders. This man was going through hell. Abused nerves were screaming in him, screaming for the only thing that would give them momentary surcease. Whiskey.

Obie Chase retrieved the glass, filled it again, set it back on the table. But he kept a hand beside it, to whisk it away if Lytell should make another grab. "See," said Obie smoothly. "Lots of whiskey, Jack. Even if you spill some." Wade Stagmire felt sorry for Lytell, but the grim need behind all this kept him adamant, harsh. In the long picture, Lytell did not count. But what he knew did—counted mightily.

"All right, Lytell . . . you've said some, too much to stop now. But still not enough. Come across with it. Who killed Harley Jacks?"

Abruptly Jack Lytell broke. The same agency that had rotted away the man's physical fiber had also burned up his mental and moral structure.

226

Fear had lived with him, ground at him, haunted him. And too much fear was its own sedative. It was a vast relief to get rid of one dread, even though that heightened another. The vital words came out of Lytell in a series of little gasps.

"Ruel Tedrow is your man! Yeah . . . Tedrow killed that rider. I was there. I saw him do it. I don't know why he did it. I never expected . . . anything like that. But Tedrow did it. He shot him, twice. Then he was going to shoot me. But for some reason he didn't. But he swore he'd kill me . . . if I spoke a word. I tell you . . . Tedrow did it! Now . . . now he'll kill me!"

Stagmire stepped back. "That does it, Obie," he said stonily. "Give him his whiskey."

Lytell gulped the liquor like it was life itself, spilling some of it down his chin. Obie poured him another shot, then looked at Stagmire.

"Ruel Tedrow, Wade. I will be damned."

"And that's why Tedrow had Mitch Caraway looking for him, Obie. No question about it. Jack Lytell is alive this minute because Caraway couldn't find him. What a basket of snakes."

"And now, Wade . . . ?" asked Obie.

"This has got to reach other ears than ours," answered Stagmire. "You'll keep Lytell here until I get back, Obie?"

"Sure. Sure I will. Who're you going after . . . Tedrow?"

"Not yet. That *hombre* will keep. I'm going after

227

Jared Hubbard. The further we dig into this thing, the deeper it gets. And I've got to have all the answers. Don't let Lytell get away from you, Obie."

"Don't worry. He'll be right where he is now when you get back," vowed Obie.

Wade Stagmire let himself out the back way, circled up an alley to the main street. It was a gray, bleak morning. Somewhere the sun was shining, but not here in Castle City. Here was a world of the ocean's dripping mists and in the distance was ocean's eternal voice, the growl of breakers foaming against the headland. And the mill saws were singing their theme of endless hunger, screaming as they chewed at the heart of still another log.

Stagmire's thoughts were as somber and chilling as the morning. He knew a harsh satisfaction over what had fallen from Jack Lytell's shaking lips, for this was the thing he was after, the thing that had brought him to Castle City. In a way it was a surprise to learn that it was Ruel Tedrow who had killed Harley Jacks, and, in another way, it was no surprise at all. Not when a man began to figure out the angles and add them up and see how they tied together and formed a bigger and more malignant picture. It was like any other puzzle, baffling until a key piece fell into place. Then it shaped up swiftly.

But—Ruel Tedrow was Jared Hubbard's right-hand man. A fact that had to be admitted. And how far would that fact lead—how far? To Jared Hubbard? Stagmire shook his head. He didn't want to believe that. He wouldn't let himself believe that. Not to Stewart Hubbard's uncle.

It was the way it had been the previous day, here in this fog-drenched lumbering town. In the dank mists everything was only half real. People abroad were phantoms, coming mysteriously out of the gray shroud, disappearing into it just as mysteriously, formless and of little substance. Stagmire paid those he met no attention at all, wrapped as he was in his grim thoughts and the depressing blanket of numbing possibilities.

He nearly bumped into a lank figure, dressed much as he himself was, a man in jeans and broad hat and spurred boots, but a man with a broke, down-at-the-heels look to him. Stagmire muttered a commonplace apology and went on, not hearing the low, startled exclamation that came from the man, nor seeing the hand that went out as though to stop him, but was jerked back before it could touch.

The lank man stared at the wind-driven blob of fog into which Wade Stagmire strode and disappeared. Then his surprise broke from him in low, startled profanity.

"I'll be damned! Wade Stagmire! It must have been him. So this is where he hightailed to! Wade Stagmire!"

Al Worter had never amounted to much, never

would amount to much. If he had possessed three times his present amount of nerve, he might have owned to a record that would have interested various officers of the law along the back trail Worter had left. But he'd never had nerve enough to leave any really broad, black marks. He'd been one who rode the fringe of the law, too weak to go fully to one side or the other. He was slippery and sly and without any discernible sense of principle. Right now he was broke and cold and hungry.

For a little time he stood there, staring into the fog. Then his sly eyes pulled down and filled with a crafty light. He spun on his heel and sought the nearest saloon. The place had just opened and was empty except for the bartender and Mitch Caraway.

The marshal was leaning against the bar, considering his first drink of the day gloomily. Mitch was tired and disgruntled over his fruit-less search for Jack Lytell, a search he was still engrossed in. Mitch was confining his search to the town's various bars, feeling certain that Lytell was bound to show up in one of them.

Al Worter looked at the bartender. "Where," he asked, "would I locate the law in this town? That is, if it has any?"

Mitch Caraway swung his broad, surly face and looked Al Worter up and down with bloodshot, protuberant eyes.

"I'm it," he growled. "What you want?"

In turn, Al Worter returned Mitch's scrutiny and liked what he saw. Here, he judged, was the sort that a man could strike up a deal with.

"I'd like to have a little talk with you," Worter said. "A private one."

"Talk about what?" demanded Caraway.

"A man."

The marshal pushed away from the bar, his drink forgotten. Maybe this fellow knew something about Jack Lytell. Mitch took Al Worter by the arm, led him to a far corner of the room, then pitched his voice low.

"You know where Jack Lytell is?"

"Jack Lytell?" Al Worter showed his surprise. "Never heard of him. I'm talking about someone else. I'm talking about a fellow named Wade Stagmire. I'm mortal certain I just saw him, out on the street."

Mitch Caraway blinked, disappointed. "You probably did," he growled. "There's an *hombre* by that name runnin' loose around here. What about him?"

"Why," said Al Worter, "he could be worth some money, to both you and me. Quite a little money."

"How in hell is that?" demanded Caraway.

The sly light in Worter's eyes deepened. "That's what I'll explain . . . later. When we've made a deal. When you agree to split even with me . . .

231

half and half. And after I've had something to eat. Right now, I'm damned hungry . . . and stone broke. You interested?"

Mitch Caraway gave Worter his best threatening stare. "If you're just cookin' somethin' up to wangle a free meal out of me, mister, you better think twice. But if you're really givin' it to me straight. I'll stake you to a breakfast."

"Friend," said Al Worter, "where a chunk of money is concerned, I never waste time on fairy tales."

Mitch Caraway made up his mind. "Come on," he said.

There was an eating house nearby and they went into it. They ordered breakfast and ate. Then Mitch Caraway, draining the last of his coffee, said: "All right. Out with it. What about Wade Stagmire?"

"Suppose," said Al Worter, "I was to tell you that Wade Stagmire is wanted . . . for murder . . . and wanted five thousand dollars' worth?"

Mitch Caraway's chin dropped and his froggy eyes bulged. "You mean that?"

"I mean it." Worter nodded. "I used to ride range back in the country where Stagmire got into this trouble. I was there when it happened. I know all about it. And I've seen the dodgers put out for Stagmire. On the hoof, I tell you, Stagmire is worth five thousand dollars' reward money. We collect him, hold him, get in touch

232

with the right persons. They'll come and get him and the money is ours. You want to deal?"

Mitch Caraway hit his hands together. "Do I want to deal! Where is this place and who are the people we get in touch with?"

Al Worter grinned slyly. "Suppose we wait a little while on that. For that's my ace in the hole and I don't show it until we've figgered out a cast-iron guarantee of my share."

Chapter Nineteen

Jared Hubbard, with the press of urgent business riding him, was early at his desk this morning. He looked up a trifle impatiently as his secretary, the mousy Miss Murdock, came in.

"Well?"

"It's that same cowboy person, Mister Hubbard. That man, Stagmire."

Miss Murdock, fearing an explosion on the part of Jared Hubbard, was amazed at the opposite result. For Hubbard spoke with obvious satisfaction when he said: "Show him in. Things I want to talk over with Wade Stagmire."

Jared Hubbard was standing, gray, impeccable, quiet, behind his desk when Wade Stagmire stepped in to face him. The lumberman nodded gravely.

"Good morning, Stagmire. Glad to see you. We've several things to discuss, you and I."

"That's correct," said Stagmire. "That's why I'm here . . . to discuss matters. And I hope the answers are fair."

Jared Hubbard stirred, disturbed and a little surprised by the somber chill in Stagmire's glance and by the undertone of suggestion in his words. "Do you know of any reason why the answers, as you call them, shouldn't be fair?"

"That depends on what you are willing to tell me," said Stagmire steadily.

Jared Hubbard's surprise deepened. "On what I'm willing to tell you? Damn it, man . . . what are you driving at?"

"Timber, for one thing. That stand of redwoods on Gib Dawson's Hester Creek property. And about Harley Jacks, one of Gib's riders, being killed there."

From that of surprise, Jared Hubbard's look became one of complete bewilderment, touched with growing anger. "I don't know what you're talking about, Stagmire. Confound it, don't look at me like that. Are you suspecting or accusing me of some crime again? The last time, as I recall, it was cattle stealing. Now you seem to be suggesting . . ."

"Mister Hubbard," cut in Stagmire, "did you order Ruel Tedrow to have that Hester Creek timber of Dawson's secretly cruised? Did you ever authorize Tedrow to try and buy that stand of timber from Dawson?"

"The answer to both questions is that I certainly did not," snapped Hubbard indignantly. "Just what are you trying to get at, anyhow?"

There could be no mistaking the sincerity of Jared Hubbard. He was aroused, his head was back, his eyes level and glinting. Wade Stagmire let out a long breath.

"I apologize," he said gravely. "I instinctively

felt from the first that you had no knowledge of this and no hand in it. Yet I had to know, to hear it from your own lips. Now I want you to come with me, Mister Hubbard. I want you to hear a mean story with your own ears, a story told by one Jack Lytell, a timber cruiser. What you will hear will jar you . . . plenty. It's going to leave you wondering about a lot of things . . . mainly men, and how much trust you can afford to place in some of them. But I know you'll thank me, later. I'd like to have you come right away, if you don't mind."

The glint in Jared Hubbard's eyes became a discerning keenness as he stared at Wade Stagmire. Here he also saw and recognized complete sincerity. And though the press of his regular work was great, he knew that he was up against something here of far greater importance. He nodded, crossed his office to a rack, and lifted down his hat and muffler and overcoat.

"Take care of things until I return, Miss Murdock," he told his secretary as he followed Stagmire out.

They went along silently, side-by-side through the fog, with Stagmire steering the way around so that they came up to the Cattleman bar by the rear entrance. Obie Chase opened the door to Stagmire's knock.

" 'Morning, Mister Hubbard," greeted Obie gravely.

Jared Hubbard acknowledged Obie's greeting with a brief nod, looked around, and then let his glance settle on Jack Lytell who, though a little steadier now, still showed plenty of evidence of his debauch. Stagmire, seeing the distaste with which Jared Hubbard viewed Lytell, spoke quietly.

"This man is Jack Lytell, Mister Hubbard. He's been over the jumps, with reason, as I think you'll come to agree."

Stagmire dropped a hand on Lytell's shoulder, spoke to him. "Mister Hubbard is going to be very interested in all that you're going to tell him, Lytell. And it's something you'll feel better about, once you get it off your chest. You've my word for it that no charge will be held against you, and I also promise that Ruel Tedrow will have no chance to get at you. All right, now. Speak up."

Lytell, now that his troubling secret had been disclosed to two men, could see no good reason why it shouldn't be heard by others. And Stagmire was right. It would be a relief to get rid of it. Lytell swung his haggard eyes around, began to speak.

"Ruel Tedrow sent out word that he wanted a special job of cruising done, and that I was to meet him in Frank Lawrey's office at Lawrey's meat cooling plant. I went there and found Lawrey and Tedrow together. Tedrow told me about the job. It was to be out at Hester Creek. I knew that the best stand of timber out there belonged to Gib Dawson and I asked Tedrow about that, asked him if Dawson was figuring on selling the stand to the Hubbard interests? Tedrow sort of side-stepped the question, and, when I asked him about it a second time, he got a little rough. He said that part of it was none of my business, that all I was to do was keep my mouth shut and cruise the timber."

Lytell paused, eyeing the whiskey bottle, but Obie Chase poured him a cup of black coffee instead. Lytell drank some of this, wiped his lips with the back of a hand, and went on slowly.

"There was something about the deal that made me wonder some. Both Tedrow and Lawrey seemed sort of restless and anxious. I guess that's when I should have backed away. But I was low on money and a job was a job. For all I knew, it could have been legitimate business Tedrow was on. Maybe some other outfit was interested in Dawson's Hester Creek timber and Tedrow was just anxious to get there first. Anyhow, I rode out to Hester Creek with Tedrow and went to work. It was Dawson's timber, all right . . . and Tedrow stayed right along with me. We'd been there a couple of hours when a few head of cattle came drifting down from the valley range to the south. Not long after, here came one of Dawson's saddle hands riding, trailing the cattle. He was a big, red-headed guy."

Lytell gulped more black coffee. Jared Hubbard had been listening intently, his glance never leaving Lytell's face. Wade Stagmire, watching both men, saw that Hubbard's dry cheeks were drawn taut and that his eyes were beginning to flash. Lytell cleared his throat.

"Sight of that cowboy upset Tedrow, plenty! He tried to duck out of sight, drawing me with him. But it was too late. This rider saw us, rode over to us, and braced Tedrow, cold. He wanted to know what the hell we were doing on Anchor property, cruising timber that belonged to Gib Dawson. Tedrow tried to put up the stall that he didn't realize we were on Anchor property, but it was a damn' thin line that didn't fool this rider at all. The redhead told us to get the hell off Gib Dawson's range and stay off. Which suited me all right, for I knew for sure by that time that I'd been pulled into some kind of shady deal."

Lytell paused again, staring straight ahead, as though looking at something he had never wanted to see and would never be able fully to forget. He shivered slightly. This time it was a short jolt of whiskey which Obie Chase handed him, and which Lytell downed with one avid gulp. It seemed to steady him enough to go on.

"I could see that Tedrow was plenty upset, and mad . . . black mad. But I had no hunch at all what he had in mind to do. If I had guessed,

I'd sure have warned that rider. But I didn't know. Anyhow, Tedrow went meek as a kitten, apparently, when all the time he was fixing to . . . to kill that rider. He kept talking smooth, apologizing all the time as he turned away. I can see now that he was doing it just to get the redhead off his guard. And that's what happened. For Tedrow had a gun in a shoulder holster. And all of a sudden he had it out and was shooting. He had maneuvered the edge of surprise he was after, all right. The rider made a grab for his own gun, but never got there. Tedrow killed him . . . shot him twice."

Telling about it, Jack Lytell was living it all over again and the shakes began to get him once more. Obie Chase poured him a little more whiskey.

Jared Hubbard's face had turned stony. But he wanted the rest of this. His voice rang harshly. "Go on. Go on, Lytell. What then?"

Lytell shrugged wearily. "We got out of there. I was too scared to think of anything but getting away from that place. I was scared that Tedrow would kill me, too. At first I was sure he was going to, for he swung his gun my way. I could see that he was more than half a mind to let me have it. I've tried to figure why he held back. Maybe it was because, over at the stable and freight yard, they knew that Tedrow and me had ridden out of town together. And if Tedrow came back alone and I never did, even though I don't amount to a damn, somebody might ask Tedrow some annoying questions. Maybe that was what Tedrow was thinking. Anyhow, he put his gun away and we headed back to our horses.

"Tedrow was cussing and damning luck and things in general and all the way back to town he was plenty rough with me, threatening me, and telling me over and over that if I opened my mouth to breathe a word of what had happened to anyone, he'd kill me. When we finally hit town, he handed over some money, told me to get myself a bottle, and forget everything. I had plenty to think about . . . and forget, all right. And for a man like me there's nothing like a quart of whiskey to help forget. . . ."

Stagmire tightened his hand on Lytell's shoulder. "Tedrow won't touch you now. We'll see to that." Then he looked at Jared Hubbard. "There it is, sir. What do you think of it?"

Jared Hubbard began to pace up and down the room. There was a strange, almost sick look about him, the look of a man who had trusted greatly and here saw that trust betrayed. He moved back and forth, back and forth, his hands clasped behind him, his bead bowed. He had been hit hard.

Gradually he mastered the first shock of this disclosure. His shoulders straightened, his head came up. The habit of a mind, long trained in logic, began to assert itself. And under the impeccable exterior of this man there was strong fiber. He ceased his pacing, faced Stagmire and Obie Chase, who had been waiting quietly for Hubbard to have this thing out with himself.

"I know that I've been listening to the stark truth," he said. "And I do not question a word of it, for there would be no purpose in Lytell bringing false witness. He saw what he saw, and that's that. You understand that this is a savage blow to me. I feel, rightly or wrongly, that I am in a way responsible. For Ruel Tedrow was my man . . . and I trusted him. A . . . a thing like this knocks a lot of the props from under a man's faith in others."

He paused, reaching inside his coat for a cigar, and he took a little time getting it going. The first mouthful of smoke seemed to steady him. He looked directly at Stagmire.

"I can understand your attitude when you came into my office this morning, Stagmire. No wonder you looked at me the way you did. For your natural assumption could only be that, inasmuch as Ruel Tedrow was my general superintendent, I must have been behind the entire affair. An entirely legitimate suspicion on your part that I do not resent in the slightest. I am very happy, of course, that you now realize that suspicion to be unfounded. I say again that I have not now, nor have I ever had, any designs on Gib Dawson's timber or ranch or cattle in any way. You believe that?"

"Absolutely, Mister Hubbard."

"Thank you, Stagmire." Jared Hubbard took another couple of turns up and down the room. "This thing has upset my thinking," he said slowly. "Ruel Tedrow must have had some purpose of his own, to do what he did, to betray my trust the way he has. I wish I knew. . . ."

"I've a theory," said Stagmire. "Maybe it hits somewhere near the truth, maybe it doesn't. It goes back quite a ways, to that rustling of cattle by Frank Lawrey and his crowd, which I once told you of, Mister Hubbard. Briefly it is like this. If enough of Gib Dawson's cattle was rustled, he'd go broke. If he went broke, he'd lose his range. If he lost his range, he'd lose that Hester Creek timber. I'm wondering if that wasn't what Lawrey . . . and Tedrow with him . . . weren't aiming at all the time?"

Jared Hubbard considered this for a moment, then nodded slightly. "That could be it. Yet . . ."

Now it was Obie Chase who spoke up. "I'm just a bartender, sitting clear on the outside of all this. But I've heard considerable talk, Mister Hubbard. For instance, I've heard that you're up against some rush orders for a lot more lumber by some of your biggest and best customers. I've heard that you're going to have to put more logging crews into the timber, speed up things at

244

the mill, and, what's most important of all, get hold of more good stands of timber, close in and easy to get at. Now then, if Tedrow and Lawrey had hold of that Hester Creek stand . . . if they could have done it without showing too much of their hand . . . maybe they might have sold it to you for a fat price. . . ."

Jared Hubbard tipped his head, looked at Obie keenly. "They might have at that," he admitted. "If they'd been able to keep me the blind fool that I've been in the past. And they probably would have, if it hadn't been for this. Somewhere in your reasoning, gentlemen, I think you're hitting close to the truth. Right now I'm anything but proud of myself. My crews eating stolen beef. This other thing . . . and I've prided myself on being able to judge the true worth of men. I wonder if I'll ever have faith in my own judgment again? Ruel Tedrow and Frank Lawrey. What a fine pair of crooks. Well, I'll take care of Mister Ruel Tedrow and his friend, Lawrey."

"No," said Stagmire quickly. "No you won't, Mister Hubbard. That little chore belongs to Anchor. Harley Jacks was one of us and we of Anchor will take care of our own. Tedrow and Lawrey belong to us."

Hubbard studied Stagmire for a moment. "We'll see. And, now that we have so many angles to consider, this may explain why that fellow Mabry tried to kill you last evening,

Stagmire. Lawrey and Tedrow could have set him after you."

Stagmire nodded. "My own thought. So you stay out of this, Mister Hubbard. You go right along as though nothing has happened. Tedrow has no idea that we know what we do. And you leave him up to me and Bill Vessels and Buck Hare."

Hubbard frowned. "I don't know as I like that, man. For a very good reason I don't want you running any further risks. I think you know the reason I speak of."

Stagmire knew, all right. Jared Hubbard was referring to Stewart Hubbard, and Stagmire knew a quick warmth toward this man for his understanding. "Any risk I take now, Mister Hubbard, will be carefully calculated, and the less because I know what to look out for."

"What about Lytell?" asked Obie Chase. "You want me to keep him here, Wade?"

"For a time, Obie. I'll come back for him later, to take him out to Anchor with me until we've done with Tedrow and Lawrey. I'll bring an extra horse for him when I get ready to leave town. Now I'm going back to your office with you, Mister Hubbard. Like you said when I first saw you this morning, you and I have something to discuss . . . and it won't be about Tedrow and Lawrey. See you a little later, Obie."

246

They went out and along the street, two men who had come to understand each other, each a strong man in his own right and, now, each with a common enemy to corner and dispose of. Jared Hubbard was silent, and Wade Stagmire respected this silence, realizing fully how shaken up Hubbard must be over the disclosures of the past hour.

Here in a way, mused Stagmire, was the same thing he'd found in Gib Dawson on that first day at Anchor headquarters, when the old cattleman had been sunk in the slough of disillusionment and bitterness over his betrayal at the hands of men he had trusted. This was the same bleak potion that Jared Hubbard was tasting at this moment. Hubbard had believed in Ruel Tedrow, trusted him utterly, and had been, over the years, building the man up to take his own place at the head of the lumber company. And now that trust and confidence was in ashes. Stagmire cleared his throat.

"I didn't enjoy doing this to you, Mister Hubbard."

Jared Hubbard shrugged. "It hurt," he admitted candidly. "But I wouldn't have wanted it otherwise. In time, and of its own accord, it was bound to have shown. And then it could have wounded more deeply, and in many other ways. It could have been too late then to mend several ghastly errors. I am deeply thankful that it comes now. It makes you wonder about men, however. Where is the truth in them?"

Inside, Wade Stagmire cringed slightly. What would Jared Hubbard think and say when he knew all about him? For he was bound that Hubbard should know. It was this that he was going to tell Hubbard about when they reached Hubbard's office.

Jared Hubbard took his half smoked cigar from his lips, looked at it, saw that it had gone dead, tossed it into the street.

"To a certain extent, now that I consider all the facts, I was armored against this. That day you first came to see me, Stagmire, about those stolen cattle, you planted a thought in my mind, whether I liked it or not. At first I was furiously angry. Then, as I cooled off and the thought kept coming back to me, I had to consider it objectively. And when I did so, I had to admit that there could have been no purpose for your visit and your charges without your having some basis of fact behind you. I think that from that moment on, I began looking at Ruel Tedrow with a brand-new discernment. And I saw things I had never seen before that made me wonder. Yet, I must also admit, I saw nothing to prepare me fully for what I learned this morning."

Through the muffling, slow-curling fog, they came up to Jared Hubbard's office building. As they paused at the door, a burly figure loomed out of the dripping mists. It was Mitch Caraway, and his heavy voice rang thickly.

"Just a minute, Mister Hubbard. There's something I figure you ought to know."

Jared Hubbard turned impatiently. "Yes? What is it?"

"This!" rasped Caraway.

With the words he had a gun jammed against Wade Stagmire's stomach, and his words hit out with a hard and vicious triumph.

"Stagmire, you're under arrest! Make one little wiggle and you get it, full in the belly. Steady!"

Wade Stagmire said not a word, but Jared Hubbard stared at the marshal with swift flaring anger. "Arrest! Caraway, what are you driving at? I believe I told you that the Price Mabry affair was finished, done with. For Mabry tried a dirty attempt at assassination, and it backfired. Put that gun away."

"No! This ain't got a thing to do with Price Mabry," exulted Caraway. "This is somethin' else . . . word that drifted in from along Stagmire's back trail. This is about another dead man, back in the country Stagmire pulled a run out from. There's a reward tied up in this, reward for a wanted man. Stagmire, I'm arrestin' you for the murder of one Dodd Evans."

Chapter Twenty

A great and bitter weariness gripped Wade Stagmire. Here it was, the thing he'd run away from. Here it was, taking him by the throat. A man was a fool to think he could leave a thing like that behind him forever. This was the thing he'd been going to talk to Jared Hubbard about. He had been going to lay all the cards on the table before Hubbard, just as he had before Gib Dawson. For he knew he owed it to Hubbard and to Hubbard's niece Stewart. Particularly to Stewart.

For, though a man might carry a scar like that on his record and say nothing about it in his everyday living with most other men, he couldn't keep it from those who had to count greatly with him. He couldn't keep it from a man like Gib Dawson, who was ready to take him at his face value, to trust him and give him a job. Nor could he keep it from Jared Hubbard, with things working out the way they were. This he had realized all along.

And so he'd intended to do things the right way, which was to tell all to Hubbard and Stewart of his own free will, to give them the truth, and then stand by their judgment. But now. Somehow this gross and venal town marshal, this Mitch

Caraway who had, by past actions, virtually admitted he was Ruel Tedrow's man—this Caraway had got hold of the word and the secret was out, and in a way that Jared Hubbard would never forgive.

Murder. That black and destroying word. It hadn't been such, but what passed for law was claiming it so. And if he submitted to this arrest, if they once had him under lock and key and helpless—then what hope for the future, what thinnest hope?

Weariness, bitter despair Wade Stagmire knew in full at this moment. Also, wild desperation and mounting savagery. He had no chance unless he made his own. And if what he had in mind didn't work, then nothing mattered anyhow.

Mitch Caraway, sure in his triumph, was grinding the muzzle of his gun, a double-acting, snub-nosed weapon, deeper into Stagmire's body.

"Your hands," he snarled, "get 'em up!"

Stagmire was standing, braced against the pressure of the marshal's gun, his hands at his side. Now he moved as though to obey Caraway's order. And in his mind he was calculating the thin splinter of time it would take for the hammer of Caraway's gun to snick back and then fall to the pressure Caraway had on the trigger. This that he intended, Stagmire knew, would be the longest and most desperate gamble of his life.

His right hand, beginning to lift, suddenly shot

across the front of his body in a hard and driving thrust. With the same move he was twisting his body back and away. The spread fingers of his right hand cradled Caraway's fist and gun, pushing them out of line. The gun blared and Stagmire felt the jerk at his clothes where the bullet cut through, and the taut, indrawn muscles of his midriff knew the touch of scorching fire. Then his left fist whipped up and smashed into Caraway's face.

Startled, half blinded by the smash of Stagmire's fist, Mitch Caraway floundered for just a brief moment. But this moment gave Stagmire time enough to wing his fist home again, and this time he was set enough to get the roll of his shoulder behind the punch. His fist caught Caraway on the side of the jaw and nearly dropped him. Caraway hauled on the trigger of his gun again and blew lead and pale flame harmlessly into the fog. He lifted a bawling, wild yell.

"This way, Lawrey! Get here . . . get your men here!"

Wade Stagmire's fist, the right this time, whistled in and cut Caraway's yell short, cutting the marshal's coarse mouth to ribbons. Caraway sagged drunkenly, dropping his gun, clapping both hands to his face in a blind gesture of protection against another of those crashing blows.

Stagmire delivered one, but not with his fists

this time. Instead, he whipped out his gun and chopped Caraway across the head with the heavy barrel. Caraway grunted and went down in a heap. Then Stagmire whirled on Jared Hubbard, who stood dazed and voiceless before the wild speed and ruthlessness of it all.

"I'm asking you not to pass judgment until you've heard all of it, Mister Hubbard. I'm asking you to give me that chance . . . !"

Then Stagmire was away, racing into the fog. He did this with the instinct of a hunted animal seeking sanctuary. For Caraway's wild yelp for help had told him that Caraway was not alone in this. Other enemies were back in that ghostly mist. Frank Lawrey and Lawrey's men. They'd be closing in now, and this time the odds were all wrong. If he wanted to live and have a fighting chance for the future, he had to run for it. And it was instinct for a saddle man to think of his horse and to head that way.

Jared Hubbard snapped out of his amazement as several men came charging up through the fog. He recognized Frank Lawrey and Ruel Tedrow, among others. He called to Tedrow.

Tedrow paid him no attention, leaning over Mitch Caraway, who had not gone completely out from the gun whipping he'd taken, but who was floundering around half stunned, trying to regain his feet. Tedrow cursed the marshal wickedly.

"Caraway, you damned bungler, you let him get

away! Which way did he go . . . which way?!" Tedrow emphasized his words with a slashing boot toe.

Mitch Caraway pointed vaguely, mumbling thickly and just as vaguely. Tedrow cursed him again, whirled away from him. "He'll try for his horse, Frank. Get after him!"

Lawrey charged off into the fog, drawing men with him. And now Tedrow whirled on Jared Hubbard, his voice harsh.

"Maybe you'll be willing to believe, now. Last evening, when he gunned Price Mabry, we tried to tell you that Stagmire was just a damned, no-good gun thrower. But you wouldn't believe!"

Jared Hubbard had full control of himself again, and his tone was ice cold as he cut into Tedrow's harangue. "I'll never believe another word you speak, Tedrow. You are a damned scoundrel, and I'll see you hung before I'm done with you."

But Jared Hubbard's last words were uttered only to the fog, for Ruel Tedrow had darted away to join in the chase. Tedrow cursed pantingly as he ran. Wasn't there any way this fellow Stagmire could be cornered and finished? Yesterday Price Mabry had had his chance and failed dismally. And after talking that failure over with Lawrey in Lawrey's office, Tedrow had told Lawrey to send for others of his crew to make sure that Wade Stagmire did not leave Castle City alive. For a mad conviction had come over Ruel Tedrow that

Wade Stagmire was a rock upon which all his carefully thought out and carefully manipulated plans were breaking up. For from the moment Stagmire had shown up at Anchor headquarters, a change had begun, gradual at first, but steadily increasing. A change that was taking Tedrow's planning apart.

Lawrey had brought in his men. They'd been gathered in Lawrey's office and Tedrow had been giving them their orders for the relentless liquidation of Stagmire, when Mitch Caraway had come hurrying in, bringing the word that a drifting rider, one Al Worter, had given him. Wade Stagmire, wanted for murder.

At the moment it had seemed the greatest break of luck in the world. Here was a weapon that Stagmire couldn't fight against. It was as simple as that. Caraway was to take him by surprise, get the drop on him, arrest him. It was an answer that would leave Tedrow and Lawrey completely in the clear, yet serve their purpose perfectly.

Well, Caraway had surprised Stagmire, gotten the drop. And even that hadn't been enough. Stagmire was loose again and, now, forewarned. Ruel Tedrow's curses trailed him as he charged on into the fog.

Back before Jared Hubbard's office, Mitch Caraway was still trying to gain his feet and hold them. The impact from Stagmire's gun barrel had been enough to put him down, partially stun him, but not enough to put him completely out. Watching Caraway, Jared Hubbard thought of a dazed hog, wallowing in the mire. He grabbed Caraway by the shoulder, hauled him to his feet.

"Listen, you blundering fool. You don't want Wade Stagmire. You want Tedrow. Understand me . . . you want Ruel Tedrow. He's the murderer. Bring me Tedrow, in handcuffs, or I'll run you out of this town forever. Bring me Tedrow!"

He gave the marshal a push and Caraway lurched blindly away into the murk, stumbling, half falling, half heavily running. And then Jared Hubbard, remembering a vital witness, hurried back toward the Cattleman bar.

Chapter Twenty-One

Wade Stagmire, racing for the livery stable, heard them come charging down the street behind him. He couldn't see them, but he could hear their running boots, clattering on the board sidewalks. And he knew now he'd never have time or the chance to get his horse. They had guessed what he was about and were set to corner him in the stable. So he cut sharply to his left along a side street, where he ran into a man who loomed suddenly in front of him. The impact knocked the man floundering and startled curses followed him and then an informing yell.

"Down this way. He went this way . . . !"

Stagmire bored on into the fog, trying to figure some answers as he ran. Denied his horse, what could he do next? He thought of the Cattleman, wondered if he could work his way there. But in the next stride he discarded this thought. That would be leading them straight to Jack Lytell, which would never do, besides getting Obie Chase into tall trouble, and he owed something better than that to Obie. There had to be some other angle.

He stopped, listened, and heard them. They were still after him. Someone in that pack had a

259

nose for the chase like a bloodhound. Stagmire drove on into the fog.

He broke clear of town with an abruptness that surprised him. Buildings had been on either side of him. Now, of a sudden, there was none. To the right and to the left there was only emptiness and the gray, cold, dripping shroud. Back and to the left, one of the mill saws, biting through a knot, screamed harshly. Out ahead the ocean boomed. Stagmire headed that way, angling a little to the right.

In a way he felt better, more secure, here in the open. Here they couldn't corner him. His thoughts took on a more orderly run. He spent no time berating the fate that had allowed that affair of the past to catch up with him. He had no idea how Mitch Caraway had learned the truth; it was enough that he had. Now he knew there was no safety for him in Castle City, not for the present at least. What he had to do was get back to ranch headquarters and there gain time to plot moves for the future where he'd have the counsel of Gib Dawson and the aid and backing of good men like Bill Vessels and Buck Hare.

He carried with him one grim satisfaction. If he never did anything else, he'd thoroughly spiked Ruel Tedrow's game as far as Jared Hubbard was concerned. Beyond doubt, Tedrow was done with Jared Hubbard. For, even though Jared Hubbard lost all faith in him, too, Stagmire knew that Hubbard could do nothing else but believe Jack Lytell's story, which meant the complete unmasking of Ruel Tedrow. To that extent, Stagmire exulted, he was still the winner.

The fog was a double-edged knife, cutting two ways. It hid him—but it also hid his pursuers, and he had no way now of telling where they were, or how close or distant. And he realized that his main problem was still to try and get hold of his horse and get out to Anchor. Neither would be easy. Tedrow and Lawrey would certainly have left somebody to guard the town livery barn. Now, reasoned Stagmire, if he could lead the bulk of the pursuit well out from town, hide his trail in the fog, and then circle back, he might be able to surprise and overpower the stable guard and get his horse after all. He had to try it, for it was his only way out.

He began to work more sharply to his right, circling. And then, abruptly, he glimpsed something more solid than fog, a shifting shadowy figure. The figure saw him and lifted the alarm yell.

"Over here . . . over here . . . !"

A gun boomed flatly, once—twice. Stagmire sensed the rip of lead whipping by him. So that was it. They would shoot him on sight. A savage game, that could be played two ways. He threw a single shot in return, holding low, and that shadowy figure went down with a wailing cry.

From a little farther back came an answering yell.

"Trautwine! Hey, Virg, you see him?"

The downed man answered. "This way, Burt. Over here!"

Stagmire backed into the fog. This brief flurry of shooting made him recall that first shot of Mitch Caraway's and the raw heat that had seared his belly muscles. How badly?

He pushed a hand inside his shirt. There was no wound, no slime of blood. Just hard and smarting flesh. Then he understood. Caraway's lead had missed him, but the flame of the marshal's gun had scorched his skin. That close had it been.

He could hear them calling back and forth now, ahead of him, to the right, and to the left. They were hemming him in. He couldn't let them get behind him, too, for then he'd be completely surrounded. He drifted back, low-crouched, hurrying.

The fog made it tough. It hid distance as well as objects. You traveled a distance through it and then you couldn't be sure how far you'd gone, for there was nothing to measure distance by. There just wasn't anything but fog. Of only one thing was Stagmire certain. He was steadily retreating closer to the ocean, for the solid roar and rumble of the breakers grew steadily louder.

A thread of panic gripped him. The unknown in front, the unknown behind him—particularly behind him. A man of the land, of the open ranges, of the mountains, Stagmire stood in awe of the sea, of its limitless reach and power. The ocean, crashing its ceaseless might against the headlands . . .

He heard voices again, men calling, close ahead. Maybe if he held his ground, got low to the earth, they'd overlook him, pass on either side of him. Then the way back to town and his horse would be open.

He dropped to one knee, waiting, head swinging, eyes peering and straining into the fog. Something wetter than that fog touched the back of his neck. A gout of wind-driven spume from the lofty crest of some rock-shattered comber. No wonder the voice of the sea had grown so hoarse and insistent. He was that close to it.

A ghostly figure to the left of him, another to his right, prowling steadily in on him. Would they see him? He crouched even lower to the earth. One of the figures gave voice, calling to the other. Frank Lawrey's voice.

"Watch yourself, Buff! He can't go back this way much farther or he'll be in the sea. Watch that he don't slip between us!"

He thought they'd overlooked him, that they'd passed him. He started to straighten up. Then a gun boomed and a clump of wet sod leaped up beside him. It was Frank Lawrey who was shooting at him. Stagmire hammered two in return, missing the first. But with the second the yell forming in Frank Lawrey's throat became just a fading sigh as Lawrey plunged down onto his face.

A gun from the other side bought in and Stagmire, dodging past Lawrey's crumpled figure, shot back, shot until his gun was empty, having no idea whether he had hit or missed. He remembered the cartridges he had put in his coat pocket and he reached for them, trying to reload as he ran.

He stumbled, for here the earth lifted in a sudden rocky slope. He recovered and went on, dropping two of the precious cartridges as he went. Then a gun blared abruptly just ahead and to his left and there was nothing for him to do but cut back and to his right once more. Someone was racing for him, closing in fast, shooting as he came.

Then the luck that had carried him this far untouched left him. A bullet struck, high on the point of his left shoulder, the shock almost spinning him off his feet. Once more he recovered and lunged on up that low slope. He topped the crest abruptly, found no support for his stumbling feet, and went headlong into a shallow, down-sloping chimney of rock beyond. He lost his gun and the impact shook him up badly, held him momentarily dazed and still. Then, as he recovered and began to struggle up, a man crashed down beside him. Instantly they were locked in struggle.

Strange how they were aware of the identity of each other. Wade Stagmire and Ruel Tedrow. Neither fog nor distance was between them now. Just the two of them, brought together in this deceptive channel of downsloping rock. The tumble had done the same to Tedrow that it had to Stagmire. Tedrow had lost his gun, too. Now here it was, raw, naked combat, hand to hand.

It was blind, it was brutal, it was elemental. It was something that must have been in the book from the very first. Two men met, looked, hated—and somewhere along the line had to have it out. No quarter here—none expected, none given. Here was the finish, one way or the other, with the ocean thundering and booming.

It was rough, very rough on Wade Stagmire. Tedrow was the heavier, the more burly, and he had seen much of rough-and-tumble conflict while climbing the ladder out of logging camps and river crew and mill crew to the position of trust and authority that Jared Hubbard had given him—and seen betrayed. And here, at this moment, Ruel Tedrow drew on every one of his black bag of dirty tricks.

He used his weight, he used his strength, he used his feet and knees, his fists. He smashed and mauled, he gouged and clawed like some great, berserk animal. He fought viciously to kill, then and there.

This rock funnel they fought in sloped ever out and down and, as they writhed and wrestled, insensate, wicked—the pull of gravity was ever at work. The sides of the funnel lifted ever higher above them, while its slope pinched in and from below them the roar of the sea grew ever deeper and more hungry.

These things were lost to Wade Stagmire. Nothing was real except this burly brute he was tangled with. Heavy fists beat at his head and face, knees ripped into his body, and shock and agony crushed and tore him. And he fought back, giving kind for kind, savagery for savagery.

Some way, unplanned, he achieved a leverage that, when he applied it, threw Tedrow off him and below him. He doubled up a leg, straightened it, smashing a boot heel into Tedrow's face. The power of this flung Tedrow back.

Stagmire followed him and from a kneeling position drove his knotted fists again and again into Tedrow's face. There was little power in Stagmire's left arm, but his right was a rawhide withe, tipped with lead, it seemed. Under the merciless and repeated impact of it, Ruel Tedrow was driven ever down and back.

Dimly, hazily Wade Stagmire marveled that he had strength enough left to raise his fist, let alone use it. Yet he did. This wild hate and desperation could do to a man. From somewhere in him these feral emotions drew on unguessed wells of energy and physical power. How long it would last, when these wells would be drained and empty, he did not know. But while he had it, he used it.

He lost track of how many times he drove that flailing right fist into Ruel Tedrow's face. That part didn't matter, anyhow. Just so long as he could keep on hammering the blows home. Tedrow seemed to go suddenly away from one of them and, when Stagmire pulled his fist back for another, there was nothing to hit at. With a stunned and bewildering suddenness, Ruel Tedrow had disappeared. He had fallen back and was gone and now, lifting up from some far-down space, came the fading hoarseness of a man's terror. But this was swiftly gone, too, caught up and dwarfed and smothered by the hissing, rumbling crash of a gigantic comber, smashing across the rocks below.

For a long, long minute, Wade Stagmire never moved. An elemental terror gripped him. Right there in front of him was nothing but fog and space, with the sea and the wet and hungry rock fangs below. Another scant yard and he would have followed Ruel Tedrow. . . .

Very, very carefully Stagmire lay back, sobbing deep breaths into his drained lungs. His brain seemed numb; his body was numb. And now there was no thread of strength in him anywhere. He had emptied the wells of that strength, emptied them completely. He lay still and the fog and the spume from the combers below drenched him.

It came back finally, some semblance of strength. It had to, or he'd have died where he lay. He went back up that rock funnel on his hands and knees, knowing a sort of stupid amazement over how far he and Tedrow had slid down it in their mad and crazy fury. He gained the top finally, crawled out onto fairly level ground once more, then lunged erect and stood, wavering on uncertain feet. What danger awaited him here?

There was no vestige of fight left in him. Somewhere along the line, it seemed, a man passed a critical point. Up to that point he was whole, but after it he was an empty shadow. His left arm was useless now. Weakness, ghastly and draining, pulled at his legs, making his knees rubbery. The muscles along his thighs felt like torn rags. He lurched ahead, straight into the fog, moving blindly.

But, queerly enough, some strength began coming back and with it a semblance of mental alertness. A building loomed ahead of him so suddenly he nearly walked into the side of it. He circled the back of this and what seemed endless numbers just like it. He had no real idea where he was going, but presently he crossed a roadway, passed by other buildings, and then, abruptly, the ammonic odor of stable refuse struck his nostrils.

Here were corrals, a freight yard. He worked through and around these things and presently he was at the back door of the livery stable. By now he knew caution and purpose and reaching senses again. He moved carefully and with full watchfulness. There seemed to be no one around. He couldn't understand this and didn't try to. He knew only a weary thankfulness.

In the end, after all the rest, it was ridiculously easy. He located his horse and riding rig. He saddled up, led his horse out the back way, pulled weakly into the saddle, and rode. The fog claimed him again, and Castle City fell steadily behind.

Chapter Twenty-Two

Castle City had known its wild moments, but never anything to match this one. A hundred rumors chased up and down the fog-shrouded streets. All sorts of wild stories were told and given credence. But in the end certain facts became known.

Jared Hubbard amassed these facts. Frank Lawrey was dead, a bullet through his heart. A rider named Virg Trautwine had a bullet-smashed leg. Ruel Tedrow had vanished, no man knew where. Wade Stagmire had likewise vanished. But Stagmire's horse and riding gear were gone from the livery barn. And it was this latter fact that Jared Hubbard, with a great sense of relief, carried home to a white-faced girl.

"There are a lot of questions to be asked and a lot of answers to be given, my dear," he told Stewart. "But of one thing, I think, we may be reasonably certain. Wade Stagmire, wherever he is, is safe enough. Now we must wait a little and depend on faith."

Other things happened. That afternoon Noyo, Gib Dawson's faithful Indian rider, slipped into town. He picked up the mail and a few other things at Sam Alexander's store, then rode away again. And although the fog lay thick and gloomy, all the balance of that day and through the following night, the next day, around noon it began to thin and scurry away before an off-shore wind that had begun to blow. The gray overcast broke and blue sky shone through. The sun came out and sodden headlands steamed and the sea lay blue-green and the combers foamed snowy white. To a waiting, taut-nerved girl this was almost like an omen.

Well along in the afternoon a lone rider came in along the Sotoyome River trail, a grizzled old man with a crutch strapped to his saddle. He rode straight to the Hubbard home, and, when he dismounted and balanced himself with his crutch, it was Stewart Hubbard who burst from the door and came running and crept into the circle of the old cattleman's free arm.

"Mister Gib . . . Mister Gib!" she wailed. "Wade . . . he's . . . ?"

"All right, honey," comforted old Gib Dawson. "Yeah, our boy is all right. He's in his bunk out at the ranch right now with Noyo fussing over him and doctoring up a few minor hurts. I tell you, the boy's all right. Now, where's that uncle of yours? Him and me, we got to have ourselves a talk . . . one that's long overdue."

Jared Hubbard met them at the door. He held out a hand, smiling gravely. It had been a long time since these two men had stood face to face. Jared Hubbard said so.

"It's been much too long, Dawson . . . and my fault. I'm very glad to see you now. And by the look of this girl of ours, I can see that you've brought some good news. Stagmire, he's safe out at your ranch?"

"He's at the ranch, Uncle Jared!" exclaimed Stewart. "And . . . safe." There were still a few tears, but these were of relief.

"I knew he would be," said Hubbard gravely. "There's a man who can take care of himself. And he certainly has cleared up a lot of things for me. Dawson, I can see you have something on your mind. Come inside and tell us about it."

Old Gib went in, his crutch creaking. Stewart swung a deep armchair up in front of the wide hearth and the cattleman lowered himself into it. He smiled up at the girl.

"Durned if this ain't more comfortable than that old rocker of mine, lass. I got to git me one like it." Then he sobered, swinging his glance to Jared Hubbard. "In case you're wondering what's become of Ruel Tedrow, he's in the ocean, somewhere. Him and Wade Stagmire fought it out on the edge of some cliff above the breakers and Tedrow went over and in. Wade was fighting for his life, so if you're holding anything against him, you can drop it now."

"I'm holding nothing against Stagmire, not even judgment," replied Hubbard quietly. "Knowing what I now know, I'd say that Ruel

Tedrow got his just deserts. Frank Lawrey, too."

Gib Dawson nodded, reached for his pipe, and got it going. "First time I ever laid eyes on Wade Stagmire there was something about him I liked. I offered him a job. Before he'd take it, he pulled a Wanted dodger out of his pocket and gave it to me, telling me to read it and then decide whether I wanted him on my payroll. That dodger was for him, for murder."

Gib's pipe wasn't drawing very well. He got out another match and freshened it. "I asked the boy to tell me all about it. He did. He admitted frankly he'd killed this feller . . . *hombre* by the name of Dodd Evans. But he did it after Evans had tried to get him in the back, dry-gulch him from the mouth of an alley. It was clear, up and down self-defense. But at the time Wade couldn't make the plea stand up because this Dodd Evans came from a powerful family that wielded plenty political power in that part of the country.

"That Evans family was after Wade's scalp, plenty. They held a stacked deck on the boy. His only chance was to skin out, which he did. Me, I believed every word Wade told me. I believed him because he's got honest eyes and because he wouldn't take the job I offered him without me knowing all about his past and passing on it, one way or the other. But me, I've lived a long time and I've learned a few things across the years. One of them is that no man can make much of his future when he has a murder charge, rightly or wrongly, hanging over him. So, on the quiet, I got Henry Carroll to head out to that River Junction country and see what he could do about clearing up the charge against Wade Stagmire."

Old Gib paused to puff reflectively for a moment or two. Jared Hubbard was in his characteristic stance, back to the hearth, hands folded behind him. Stewart had dropped down, cross-legged, beside the cattleman's chair, one slim shoulder leaning against Dawson's knee. Neither she nor her uncle spoke, waiting for Dawson to continue. Dawson cleared his throat.

"I figgered that Henry would get some kind of action, him being plenty shrewd that way. But I never expected him to get action so quick. Yesterday I sent Noyo into town after some things. He brought out the mail and there was a letter for me from Henry Carroll. Jared, I want you to read it."

Dawson brought the letter from a pocket, handed it over. Hubbard read it, silently the first time, and then a section of it aloud, after glancing down at Stewart.

" 'Remember what I said about a closet full of skeletons, Gib? Well, this one was stacked to the ceiling. I found plenty of people who'd been pushed around at one time or another who didn't exactly love this Evans family. And those good folks furnished me the keys to that closet.

I rattled the bones and the Evanses came to their fodder, quick! Evidence of the shooting affair was reviewed and furnished the answer as it should have been in the first place, clear cut self-defense. The charge against Wade Stagmire has been quashed, definitely withdrawn. The Evans family doesn't love me, but the local sheriff does. We had a drink together just before I sat down to write this letter. For he's also fed up with being pushed around by the Evanses. . . .' "

Chapter Twenty-Three

Jared Hubbard ceased reading, for the rest of the letter did not matter. He glanced again at Stewart and her lovely gray eyes were shining.

Hubbard folded the letter carefully, handed it back to Gib Dawson. "Thanks for showing me that, Gib. It makes me happy . . . for many reasons. A certain chapter in all our lives has been closed. Now we can look at other . . . and better chapters ahead. It seems I owe you for a lot of Anchor beef that my crews have been eating, unbeknownst to me. Make out your bill and I'll pay it."

"You don't owe me a dime, Jared," growled old Gib. "It was worth every cent of it to get so many trails cleared up. But if you're interested in it, I am going to soak you plenty for that stand of redwood timber of mine along Hester Crick. I understand you're kinda hard put for timber that's close in and easy to get at and I been thinking that I got no right to hang on to something I'll never use. You do need timber pretty bad, don't you?"

"I thought I did," acceded Hubbard. "But now I'm not so sure. You see, Gib, of a sudden I've got a different slant on a lot of things. Call it the correct appreciation of the real values in life.

277

I find of a sudden that there are a lot of things much more important than just getting bigger and bigger. A man's a fool to lose himself so deeply in his business he can't see anything else. So, I've just about decided that the Hubbard Lumber Company is big enough as it is. I'm going to lose some good accounts perhaps, by not expanding, but I'll get others, enough to keep the mill busy. All my life I've thought of nothing but work. Now I've a great yen to slow up and look around a little."

"Man," exclaimed Dawson, "now you're talking sense!"

"I think so." Hubbard smiled. "I've just seen greed turn men bad, Gib . . . so I want no part of it. I trusted a man and believed in him and found that greed had made a complete rascal of him. That has forced me to take a good look at myself. I wonder if I haven't been a little greedy, too. I think so. So now I want to wipe out that stain."

"Uncle Jared," interrupted Stewart, "you shouldn't say that. No man could have been more generous than you've been, to me and to others. I . . ."

"I was thinking of something else, my dear," broke in Hubbard. "I was thinking of how much I've taken from this great forest of redwoods and suddenly I'm more than a little ashamed of myself. For these great trees weren't put here just for my benefit or the individual benefit of any other one man. Gib, about that Hester Creek stand of yours . . . I've never seen that grove, but I hear it is something to look at."

"Finest grove of trees I ever laid eyes on," vowed Dawson. "And I've seen a lot of them."

"Well, here is what I'd like to do with that grove," Hubbard said. "There are a lot of future generations coming along behind us, Gib. I'd like to feel that through my efforts there was one outstanding grove of redwoods for those generations to look and marvel at, that had never been touched by axe or saw. A spot where people could go and stand in awe and perhaps get a clearer conception of the handiwork of the Almighty. I think that would be good for them, Gib . . . and good for us, too . . . and I feel that they would thank us for it. So here's what I propose. I'll buy that Hester Creek grove from you and set it up as a sanctuary, something to be kept untouched by man through all the future, just as God planted those great trees and kept them. What do you say?"

It was Stewart who answered first. She jumped to her feet and hugged her uncle mightily. "That's the grandest thought you ever had, Uncle Jared."

"Only one thing wrong with it," growled Gib Dawson. "I'd never sell timber of mine for such a cause." And then, when Stewart whirled on him with a little unbelieving gasp of dismay, his deep, fierce old eyes twinkled. "No," he repeated, "I wouldn't sell it. But I'd give it. And that's how we'll do it, Jared . . . you and me. I'll give the grove and you handle all the rest of the details." And then he added, with another twinkle: "Don't that make me grand too, lass?"

It seemed that it did, for he got his hug, also.

"One final angle," said Jared Hubbard. "I'm going to need beef to feed my crews. Think you can handle the contract, Gib?"

"Maybe I can't. But my help can . . . Wade Stagmire and Bill Vessels and Buck Hare. You talk it up with them and you'll find you got yourself a deal."

"I'll do that tomorrow," Hubbard said. "You're staying the night with me and Stewart and first thing in the morning we go back with you to your ranch. Because Stewart would go, I think, even if I didn't." He looked at her fondly and smiled.

"Why, yes, Uncle Jared, I would," she said steadily. Then she flushed rosily.

Hubbard's smile widened. "Knows her mind, that girl does. Gib, how about a little nip?"

Gib Dawson grinned. "Now that's man talk I approve of."

Chapter Twenty-Four

The valley of the Sotoyome River, fresh and dewy in the morning sunlight. A cow bawling in sheer, full-fed contentment in the distance. A bluebottle fly buzzing up against the growing warmth of the bunkhouse roof.

These things Wade Stagmire was aware of as he stirred in his blankets and grunted over the protest of stiffened, beaten muscles. A twinge of pain stabbed the tightly bandaged point of his left shoulder. He eased carefully around, swung his feet to the floor, and grunted again at the effort of sitting up.

Noyo came in and began to protest furiously. "Not good . . . not good, Wade! You stay. . . ."

Stagmire shook his head. "Things to do, Noyo . . . people to see." He was a little somber about this. Then he added: "Give me a hand with my duds. Soon as I get up and moving around, I'll be all right."

Noyo realized that argument was useless, but he had his say. "Stubborn . . . like hell. No sense at all."

Stagmire grinned crookedly. "Absolutely right on both counts, Noyo. Chuck me my boots."

Noyo did, and growled: "Who you want to see?"

"People. The Hubbards, mainly. I got to square

myself with them. *Ow-w-w!* That shoulder is plenty sore."

"What you expect?" snorted Noyo. "You get sick again, Noyo feed you strychnine."

Stagmire hitched himself up and down the bunkhouse, working out the stiffness and swearing softly at the effort. He stopped and took a look in the small shaving mirror hung on the wall. He saw plenty of dark bruises.

"I look like hell," he gloomed. "Where's Gib and Bill and Buck?"

"Bill and Buck, they out working. Gib in town."

"In town. That's a tough ride for Gib."

Noyo shrugged. "Tough ride, tough man. Good man, too."

Stagmire washed his face with one hand, at the basin and bench outside the door. He used the towel gingerly. But surface soreness did not count and inside he was loosening up. He realized he was hungry and said so.

Noyo said: "I saved your breakfast."

They started over to the cook shack together, and then turned at the sound of hoofs. Three people came riding up from the river trail. Gib Dawson, Jared Hubbard, and—Stewart.

Gib Dawson yelled at him with mock harshness. "Durned young idiot! Why ain't you staying in bed?"

Stagmire went slowly to meet them. "Too fine a day to stay in bed, Gib," he answered in kind.

Then he sobered, watching Stewart, and waiting.

She swung down from her sorrel and came directly to him.

Jared Hubbard jabbed Gib Dawson in the ribs and jerked his head toward the ranch house. They went off that way, Gib's crutch making its measured creaking.

Stagmire watched Stewart Hubbard silently. He thought that she had never looked lovelier. She was twisting her hands a little.

"Wade," she murmured. Then, as his silence continued, she asked: "Haven't you anything to say to me?"

"I could say a million things . . . if I had the right." He spoke very gravely. "But after all that's happened, and after what you know about me now, I'm not sure that I have that right."

She came very close to him. "You're the same man you always were. Nothing has changed you, nothing ever will. And so, nothing else matters."

He took her hands, looked deeply into those shining gray eyes, and what he saw there made him realize beyond all doubt that nothing else did.

In the doorway of the ranch house, Gib Dawson and Jared Hubbard paused to watch for a moment. Then Gib grinned broadly.

"Jared, how about a little nip?"

"Now that," said Jared Hubbard heartily, "is man talk I approve of."

About the Author

L. P. Holmes was the author of a number of outstanding Western novels. Born in a snowed-in log cabin in the heart of the Rockies near Breckenridge, Colorado, Holmes moved with his family when very young to northern California and it was there that his father and older brothers built the ranch house where Holmes grew up and where, in later life, he would live again. He published his first story—"The Passing of the Ghost"—in *Action Stories* (9/25). He was paid ½¢ a word and received a check for $40. "Yeah . . . forty bucks," he said later. "Don't laugh. In those far-off days . . . a pair of young parents with a three-year-old son could buy a lot of groceries on forty bucks." He went on to contribute nearly six hundred stories of varying lengths to the magazine market as well as to write numerous Western novels. For many years of his life, Holmes would write in the mornings and spend his afternoons calling on a group of friends in town, among them the blind Western author, Charles H. Snow, who Lew Holmes always called Judge Snow (because he was Napa's Justice of the Peace in 1920-1924) and who frequently makes an appearance in later novels as a local justice in Holmes's imaginary

Western communities. Holmes produced such notable novels as *Somewhere They Die* (1955) for which he received the Spur Award from the Western Writers of America. *Desert Steel* (Five Star, 2011) marked his most recent appearance. In these novels one finds the themes so basic to his Western fiction: the loyalty that unites one man to another, the pride one must take in his work and a job well done, the innate generosity of most of the people who live in Holmes's ambient Western communities, and the vital relationship between a man and a woman in making a better life.

Center Point Large Print
600 Brooks Road / PO Box 1
Thorndike, ME 04986-0001 USA

(207) 568-3717

US & Canada:
1 800 929-9108
www.centerpointlargeprint.com